BEST INTENTIONS

Maggie spends Sundays and Tuesdays helping to serve tea and hot meals to the homeless in her city, though her volunteer group must contend with vandals burning the facilities down. Then she meets the handsome and mysterious Cliff, who makes no secret of his attraction to her as she serves him tea — but is he one of the homeless, or does he have a deeper agenda? Sparks fly as Maggie and Cliff get to know each other; and then Maggie's work throws her into a life-threatening situation . . .

SARAH SWATRIDGE

◆

BEST INTENTIONS

Complete and Unabridged

LINFORD
Leicester

First published in Great Britain in 2020

First Linford Edition
published 2020

A catalogue record for this book is available
from the British Library.

ISBN 978–1–4448–4433–7

Published by
Ulverscroft Limited
Anstey, Leicestershire

Set by Words & Graphics Ltd.
Anstey, Leicestershire
Printed and bound in Great Britain by
T. J. International Ltd., Padstow, Cornwall

This book is printed on acid-free paper

1

It was almost 5 p.m. when Maggie drove into the city centre. It was Sunday. Most of the shops were now closed or closing. Many were boarded up, perhaps for good. However, the town was full of lights, but even their brightness did nothing to cheer up the concrete, litter and graffiti. Maggie had always preferred the countryside where she lived to the towns and cities.

Cheerfully she sang along to the radio in her little Citroën C3. It was the beginning of another new year and a time to feel positive. Being rich, attractive and in her mid-twenties, she had everything to look forward to.

Her heart sank as she reached the old centre of town, away from the new shopping precinct. It was always dark here because of the shadow of the huge multi-storey car park that now loomed over the old marketplace. A few street lamps were reflected in the puddles, but they didn't light up the gloomy corners and doorways where many spent their nights.

She checked her watch, and just as she did so, the five o'clock news began, so she knew she was on time. Dee should be here; she was always here, thought Maggie.

Something was wrong. She had expected to find a gathering of the city's homeless, but the place was deserted.

Maggie parked, and as she looked up, she realised why. She opened her car door, and instantly could smell the smoke still lingering in the air. The little cabin where for the past two years she'd served tea to those sleeping rough or in council bed and breakfast accommodation had been completely burnt down.

She approached the little shelter slowly hoping her eyes were deceiving her, but even in the drizzling rain she could only make out its shell. Not only burnt, she thought, but ransacked too.

None of the supplies or the hot water urn were visible.

This was the third time in the last six months. She thought she knew who was responsible, but had no proof. There were no CCTV cameras around. There was nothing here worth stealing, so the police and council told her.

The rain moved up a notch from drizzle to something heavier. Maggie reached for her mobile and rang Dee.

'It's happened again,' she said.

'I'm so sorry,' said Dee. 'I'm on my way. You wouldn't believe it! I loaded up the car as usual, only to discover a flat tyre. Luckily my son's here, so he's lent me his car while he fixes mine. Isn't he wonderful?'

'The shed's gone, burnt again,' said Maggie.

'Burnt? Again?' said Dee in disbelief. 'Maybe this time someone will have seen something,' she said weakly, because they both knew no one would own up, or dare to be a witness.

'Anyway,' said Maggie, forcing herself

to sound cheerful, 'business as usual.'

'I'll be with you in a few minutes,' said Dee. 'Bye for now.'

At that moment, a big white van appeared and crunched to a halt beside Maggie's little Citroën. She put away her phone and greeted another volunteer.

'Paulo! Am I glad to see you!' said Maggie. She could see he was looking through her toward where their tea bar had been.

'You should not be here on your own, alone,' said Paulo in his broken English.

'I'm not on my own anymore. You're here,' said Maggie quickly. 'And Dee's on her way. She had a flat tyre.'

'And that's happened before. They know where she lives,' said Paulo, showing a little of his temper.

'Don't say that to her, you'll only make her worry,' warned Maggie as she helped Paulo unload his van.

They didn't have a table, but Paulo did have some wooden pallets in the back of his van, so they put one on top of a rubbish bin to use as a table for Dee, and piled a couple more on some old crates for Maggie to use.

'I've got tea bags and things in my car,' said Maggie. 'But I've only got two flasks of boiling water.'

'I've got some too,' said Paulo, 'I bring them to you. I have only three.'

As if by magic, while they were setting up their makeshift stall, their regular 'customers' appeared. They were wrapped up well to keep out the cold and the rain.

Dee arrived a few minutes later with her casserole dishes of hot stew which she served out to the needy. She and her church volunteered to do this once every week.

Every Sunday morning, Dee and a few friends chopped vegetables and cut meat. They popped them in the slow cooker and went off to their local service. There were six double sockets in Dee's kitchen and sometimes each one was used. The aroma of home-cooked stew was wonderful.

5

'I've got some sleeping bags and clothes when you've got a moment,' said Maggie. Dee nodded. 'Tea or coffee?' Maggie asked an elderly gentleman with a thick black coat and long straggly beard.

'Tea, love. Two sugars.'

'Here you are,' she said, carefully handing a polystyrene cup to him. 'Tea? Coffee?' she asked as she made eye contact with the next person standing around their little table.

'No soup, love?' asked a man in a checked jacket.

'Sorry,' said Maggie, tilting her head to one side in the direction of the burnt-down shed. 'We've only tea or coffee today. We've had a bit of a setback.'

'Coffee then,' said the man. 'I don't suppose anyone saw what happened?'

'No one's said anything to me, but if you hear anything, please let me know.'

A teenage lad asked her for two teas. She noticed he didn't have a coat or even a jacket. The forecast said the temperature was due to plummet.

'When you've had your drink, see

Dee over there; she's got some warm clothing you can look through.'

'Thanks,' said the young man. Maggie watched as he disappeared to the edge of the crowd and handed one cup of tea to a young girl. Maggie hadn't seen either of them before and wondered if they were just passing through or here to stay.

Maggie kept her head down for the next ten minutes or so as she poured and distributed the hot drinks. They were just getting to the end of the boiling water when she looked up to gauge whether it was worth going to beg for more hot water at one of the local restaurants. One or two of the cafés locally were friendly, but most actively didn't want to encourage the homeless to gather in their area.

'I think we'll be all right,' said Maggie to Paulo. Most people had eaten some of Dee's hot stew and drunk at least one hot drink. The rain was still coming down, making the little bags of sugar damp, but no one cared. Little things like that were not really important. Maggie put a newspaper over the top of the sugar to keep it dry.

'Excuse me a minute,' Maggie said to Paulo. She fished out her car keys and opened up her car boot. It was full of warm jumpers, blankets, and a few sleeping bags. She took them over to Dee, who always took charge of handing things out. She mentioned the young lad with no coat and nodded in his direction. Maggie returned to her tea bar position and asked if anyone else wanted more tea.

'Can I pour you a tea or coffee?' she asked, and looked up to see who still needed serving. Her eyes met with someone new. Even in the dim light, she could tell he was strikingly handsome. He stood upright too, unlike many of the men who hunched their shoulders against the cold and the bitter deal they'd been handed. He stood tall and proud, comfortable in his own skin. It made him stand out. 'Can I get you a tea or coffee?' Maggie asked again.

'Only if you've enough,' he said, stepping forward.

Maggie shook her flask. 'There should be enough, but we're almost done now.'

'A coffee would be lovely,' he said, and pulled off his gloves to help himself to sugar. 'I'd be really grateful if you could take off your gloves for a moment,' he asked softly. He had a slight accent. Maggie wasn't sure where he was from, but it was gentle and educated.

Maggie took off her fingerless gloves and stuffed them in her pocket, without making a comment. She didn't look up, but just continued to make him a coffee.

'What's that all about, governor?' asked one man who'd been standing nearby.

'Just wanted to see if she had a wedding ring,' the handsome man answered, which caused much laughter all around. Maggie pulled her gloves back on over her ringless fingers, and poured the last of the hot water from her flask into a cup.

'Sorry, that's the last one,' she said, and looked at Paulo, who nodded. He too had little water left.

'I have about one more only,' he confirmed.

Maggie made sure she kept her eyes down, away from the newcomer. She had no wish to get involved with anyone, much to her mother's annoyance.

She handed him his drink without making eye contact. He was too gorgeous to look at. She did notice his fingernails were clean and his hands well cared for. If he was sleeping rough, at least he still managed to look after himself. Some were beyond caring.

'Thank you,' he said.

'What's your name?' asked one of the other guys. 'I haven't seen you around here before.'

'Cliff,' said the newcomer. He put down his coffee and offered to shake the man's hand.

'Dave.'

Paulo collected up the flasks and began to head off to find a good

Samaritan to fill them with boiling water. Dee had now gone off to Pret A Manger to collect up their unsold sandwiches, which they kindly donated each Sunday.

'I don't mind going,' offered Maggie.

'No problem,' said Paulo. 'I'll try The Pizza Place. They were good to us before.'

'I'd send a pretty woman,' suggested Cliff. 'She's bound to have more luck.' Again, there was a general chuckle. Maggie could feel herself blushing.

Paulo hesitated for a moment, but then carried on with his mission.

Maggie picked up a bin liner and began to collect up the empty cups and pop them in the bag. She preferred to keep herself busy. She could feel she was being watched.

As Maggie neared the young lad and the girl, she offered them a friendly smile. It was then that she got a closer look at the young girl. She too didn't wear a coat or jacket and was visibly shivering.

But what was more striking was that she looked so familiar. Maggie paused for a moment, trying to recall where she'd seen the girl before. She was certain it wasn't at the tea bar or the church hall.

'Don't forget to see Dee,' Maggie told them. 'She might have a raincoat and some jumpers you could make use of.'

'Thanks,' said the young boy again, but neither of them moved toward Dee, who was now handing out sleeping bags and blankets.

Maggie couldn't stop herself as she collected up the last of the polystyrene cups. Her eyes were drawn back to Cliff.

He was tall enough to be a policeman, she thought. She looked down at his feet. Policemen, even in plain clothes, usually wore sensible black regulation shoes. He wore sturdy walking boots. It was not conclusive, thought Maggie; he could be police, but then again, he could be homeless. Over the years, she'd heard so many tragic stories of people losing their jobs through no fault of their own. Then, without an income, they lost their accommodation and relied on strangers for food and comfort.

As she watched, she realised with delight that he was a listener. Dave was telling him one of his long stories. Cliff nodded every now and again to encourage him, but didn't interrupt. People needed to feel they were being heard. It made them feel they were still valued, even if they didn't happen to have anywhere to live at the moment.

She couldn't help but be interested in him. His good looks, his easy manner. She liked the way he stood proud; so many men here had lost that. She wondered what his story could be.

The rain was easing off just as Paulo returned with two flasks of boiling water. Dee was now offering sandwiches and wraps thanks to Pret A Manger.

Maggie poured more hot drinks so people could wash down their food. She stole a glance and noticed Cliff had not taken any, nor did he want another drink. Pride, she thought, could keep a man hungry.

'Are you sure you won't have another drink?' asked Maggie. 'We're nearly out of water again, and that'll be it for this evening.'

'Do you do this every Sunday?' asked Cliff.

'Maggie does Sundays and Tuesdays,' interrupted Paulo with a grin.

'So, it's Maggie is it?' said Cliff, offering her his hand.

It would be rude not to shake it, thought Maggie, even though she was trying to clear away and get their meagre provisions out of the rain.

Maggie accepted his hand, and just for a moment looked up into his lovely blue eyes. They sparkled with a zest for life. Cliff held her hand and her eye contact until Maggie felt she had to withdraw.

Maggie had to physically look up to Cliff, she being only 5'2" and him being about six foot. He had fine black hair and dazzling blue eyes, while she seemed the complete opposite, with long dark curly locks and hazel eyes.

'Can I help?' he asked.

He had the beginnings of a beard, dark, like his hair. It was a little more than being unshaven for just a few days. Maggie wondered how long he'd been living rough.

She nodded toward the pallets as she began to pack up the makeshift table. Cliff bent forward to help her, and together they lifted the pallets into the van to be used another time.

Just as people had come out of the woodwork when they set up the table, now everyone disappeared again. The teenage couple had gone. They hadn't approached Dee for warm clothes or blankets.

Maggie always wondered where they went. It was still early and still wet, but she would never ask. She didn't feel it was her place to pry into other people's private lives.

'We usually serve from that wooden cabin,' explained Maggie to Cliff the newcomer, looking at the burnt-out hut. 'But there must have been a fire.'

'I heard someone talking about that earlier,' Cliff told her. 'It was fine this morning, apparently.'

'Did anyone say they saw anything?' asked Maggie hopefully, looking up into his eyes.

'I didn't hear of any witnesses,' admitted Cliff.

'Unlikely if we ever will,' said Maggie with a sigh. 'This is the third time it's happened. I doubt if we'll buy another cabin this time.'

'But you obviously do a good job,' Cliff told her. He seemed surprised at her reaction not to rebuild.

'Oh, we'll carry on. Maybe we'll get a mobile van or something. I don't want to pry,' said Maggie, 'but have you got somewhere to stay tonight?'

'Don't worry about me,' said Cliff, 'unless you're inviting me to share your bed! Now that I couldn't refuse!' He gave her a boyish, cheeky grin. Maggie's heart did a little leap. He looked even more dashingly handsome when he grinned like that.

Paulo was locking up his van. 'I go now,' he announced. 'You OK?' he asked Maggie.

'Yes, I'll be off too,' said Maggie. 'See you Tuesday.' Then she turned to Cliff. 'Do let me know if you hear anything else about the cabin. I'm not really expecting any results, but if we could find out who did it and even better, prove it, that would be something.'

'Will I see you here again on Tuesday?' asked Cliff with another of his melting smiles.

'I'll see you on Tuesday,' replied Maggie, returning his smile, but trying to sound cool. She felt an unexplained warm glow in her heart. She was looking forward to Tuesday evening already, despite the weather forecast showing possible sleet. 'On Tuesdays,' she explained, 'we meet in the church hall.' She pointed over the road to a large church with a small hall tagged on to the side of it. 'But if you need a hot meal tomorrow night, then try the Salvation Army.'

Maggie drove away from the city centre with mixed feelings. She felt pleased she'd been able to be useful, but was cross with herself for feeling the way she did about Cliff. She had to admit to herself that she was attracted to him.

She tried to imagine what it must be like to be living in bed and breakfast accommodation or in a hostel. From what she'd heard from some of the women, they were scary places to be living in, especially with children crying all the time, fights between the girls, and any possessions being taken. Nothing, it seemed, was sacred, even your toothbrush!

Instead of going straight home, Maggie called in at All Saints Church. Evensong was just finishing. They had an early service during the winter.

Maggie waited at the back of the church until all the congregation had

18

gone. It struck her how warm and inviting it was in church after the cold damp night air she'd been out in. She often mused what she would do if she were ever homeless. She knew she would head for the nearest church and was confident that someone would take her in and look after her, but then, she'd spent her life in and out of church and felt very much at home in one.

'It's good to see you,' said Robert, the vicar, and Maggie's dad. 'You look happy!'

'Do I?' asked Maggie in surprise. 'I can't think why. The tea cabin's been burnt down again and I really don't know what to do next.'

'Were you able to serve any teas?'

'Yes, I'd taken two flasks of water, and Paulo always brings things in his van. I don't know what we'd do without him. He's so good and kind. And Dee was there too with her fantastic stew. If whoever burnt the cabin down was hoping we'd go away, they would have been disappointed, but . . . '

'What?'

'Well, Dee's tyre was flat again, and it just seems such a coincidence. I do worry that whoever is doing this is going to get personal.'

'Do they know where you live?' asked Robert. His brows met together, and this was a sure sign that he was concerned.

'I don't think so,' admitted Maggie. 'I've never thought anyone was following me, and I often do something else after serving at the tea bar, before going home — mainly so Mum isn't suspicious.'

'You really ought to come clean with her,' said Robert, not for the first time. 'You know how I feel about this. I'd much rather everything was out in the open and honest.'

'You know Mum, she'd only worry,' said Maggie. 'But you're right, it would be better to be open and honest. I've tried to tell her,' admitted Maggie, 'but I always back down and find some excuse not to. I promise I'll make a real effort to tell her and explain why I do it.'

'Then the least I can do is reassure your mother that you have a good team around you, and although Paulo isn't a body guard, he wouldn't let anyone harm you.'

'No one will harm me. I never, ever, feel threatened or in danger,' said Maggie with feeling. 'In fact, there are a lot of real gentlemen out there. They just happen to be homeless at the moment.'

'I'm sure your mother will just be glad you're not bringing them all home to live in Haddon Hall. Now that she would find difficult.'

'Like you using The Vicarage as rent-free accommodation for young people so they can save up enough for a deposit on their own home?' teased Maggie, knowing that was exactly what her father had done, with the church's backing and the parish council's reluctant consent, when he'd married the wealthy Nancy Haddon of Haddon Hall.

A thought struck her as she tidied up

a pile of hymn books. She felt that tonight she'd been protected, and not just by her faith. It was a silly thought, and she dismissed it straight away, but somehow she felt that Cliff would have protected her if she had needed it tonight. She'd been aware that he'd been watching her, almost as much as she'd been watching him. What a pair they were! Perhaps he was in the police force after all.

'I think I'm beginning to worry,' said Robert with a serious look on his face.

'Honestly, Dad, I never give my full name or address to anyone. I really don't think anyone knows anything about me, but I'll be careful.'

'Maybe I should pick you up next week,' suggested Robert. 'Then they won't even be able to get your car registration number.'

'What about evensong?' asked Maggie, surprised at her father's concern. This sort of thing was always happening and he'd never seemed too bothered about it before.

'Perhaps one of the church wardens would do the last bit and lock up?'

'Don't worry, I'll be fine. But if you hear of a mobile catering van going cheap, then you'll let me know, won't you?'

'Are you going home now?' asked Robert.

'Are you?'

'I've got a few phone calls to make, and a couple are coming to talk about their wedding, so I'll be about an hour or so.'

'Maybe they'd like me to do their flowers?' asked Maggie.

'I'll certainly give them one of your cards,' laughed Robert. 'Why don't you go and put the kettle on, and I'll come and join you in the office.'

Maggie did as her father suggested. She made them both a mug of tea. She washed up a few cups from an earlier meeting and tidied up the piles of leaflets that littered the table outside his study.

She waited until the bridal couple

arrived, and let her father introduce her as his daughter and local florist. Once they had her business card, she kissed her father goodnight and made her way home.

Just as she was getting into her car, she realised where she'd recognised the young girl she'd seen with the teenage boy tonight.

Her best friend, Angela, had a younger sister, Jessica. She'd not coped with the death of their mother and had been no help with their father. Angela and Jess had argued one day a few months ago and Jess had walked out and had never returned.

But it was not her best friend, or her father, or the engaged couple who filled her thoughts as she drove the short journey from All Saints Church to Haddon Hall, but the stranger, Cliff, whose handsome good looks and gentle manner were foremost in her mind.

2

Maggie spent the morning working at the food bank. Volunteers and drivers would collect up donations of food from local supermarkets or from community groups and drop it off at the bank and Maggie and her team would sort the food, checking the use-by dates.

Later they would make up food parcels for the drivers to deliver to needy people in the area. If they were short of drivers, Maggie would muck in. She liked meeting people, but felt she never had enough time to listen to their stories.

After a full day at the food bank, Maggie hurried along to the church hall to see what she could do to help. A team of volunteers were already cleaning and chopping vegetables by the time she arrived. She put on an apron and began to peel a mountain of potatoes.

In theory there were lots of willing helpers, but in practice she only ever saw the same people each week. They were a friendly lot. She enjoyed the banter and liked to hear what everyone had been up to. She was pleased that she didn't feel she had to confess about her own week, unless she had a funny or heart-warming story to share. After all, they were here to do a job, and there was a hot supper to be prepared.

The church hall was cold. The heating had been on an hour, but the building was still chilly.

'It'll soon warm up when it's full of people,' said Maggie cheerfully. She stamped her feet to wake up her toes. She had two layers of socks and had spent the last hour in the steamy kitchen, but still her feet felt like blocks of ice.

'That smells good,' said George, the church warden. 'What are you serving up today?'

'Cabbage and potato soup,' replied Maggie, giving the huge pan another stir. 'No meat today, I'm afraid. We've only had donations of vegetables this week.'

'I'm sure it will fill a hole, and that's what is important,' said George, helping himself to a cup of tea from the large brown teapot. 'I'll just down this and then go and open up.' He glanced at the clock.

Maggie looked at the window. It had been trying to snow all day and there was a bitter wind.

'You take your time,' said Maggie, offering him the biscuit tin. 'I don't mind opening up. I'd rather do that than leave people out in the cold.'

George only hesitated for a moment before reaching in his pocket for the keys.

Maggie struggled to open the heavy wooden door, but eventually managed it only to find a small group of men huddled together in the doorway.

A powdery shower of snow was falling and beginning to cover the local roof tops and cars. Maggie stepped back to let the men inside in the warm. She waited at the entrance, fascinated by the falling snow. It was unlikely to settle for long, but even a small amount could transform one of the poorest areas of a city, like this one, into a place of beauty, when covered in a blanket of pure white snow.

She shivered and realised she really ought to be inside doing the job she came here to do.

It always surprised Maggie that no matter what they served up, no one was ever critical. They were always so grateful. It was one of the best bits of her job.

Maggie was fortunate that over the years she had mixed with lots of people from all sorts of different backgrounds. Some had everything and still wanted more, while others had nothing and were so grateful for a bowl of home-made cabbage and potato soup.

She'd been serving for about ten minutes before she happened to glance up and her eyes fell, as if drawn, to the tall, dark figure hovering by the door.

Maggie's heartbeat quickened. She'd been hoping he would come. Her mind had been on Cliff more than anything else since Sunday. Even her mother had noticed, and commented about her being 'lost in a world of dreams'! If only her mother had known the truth.

Following her recent conversation with her father, she had vowed to come clean with her mum and confess that twice a week she did voluntary work for a Christian charity helping the homeless in the local city. She knew she would have to reassure her mother, but eventually she would come round to the idea and might even be proud of her only daughter.

All in one moment, she'd been so distracted that she'd picked up a plate instead of a bowl and begun to ladle soup onto it.

'Oh dear!' said Maggie with a light laugh as she tipped the soup back into the pan and slipped the plate into the bowl for washing up.

The next twenty minutes were taken

up just serving soup and bread to anyone who requested it. Maggie kept one eye out for Jessica and the teenage boy. She had to make sure it was really her before getting Angela's hopes up.

There was then a lull. Patrick had finished his soup and was sitting at one of the trestle tables. He leaned back, looking for all the world as though he'd dined on oysters and champagne. He wore a contented smile as he brought out his harmonica and gave everyone a cheerful Irish tune.

Maggie turned off the heat and covered what remained of the soup with a lid. She hesitated at the kitchen door, wondering whether she should remove her apron, but then decided against it and went to sit at the tables and chat to her 'guests', checking that they had accommodation for tonight — especially tonight, due to the falling snow.

There was still no sign of Jessica or the young lad. She felt sure she'd recognise them both if she saw them again.

As Maggie stepped into the hall, her eyes were drawn again, like a magnet, towards Cliff. He'd come a little further into the hall, but still lingered near the back.

Maggie braced herself. She knew if she didn't approach him, he could turn and go and she'd be cross with herself if she'd missed an opportunity to talk to him.

'Hello Cliff,' said Maggie. 'We've got some homemade cabbage and potato soup and bread tonight. Would you like a bowl?'

'I'm fine, thanks,' said Cliff. 'Do you always remember people's names, Maggie?' he asked, putting the emphasis on her name.

'I do try to,' she said quietly.

Brian, one of the volunteers, was going round with a tray of hot drinks. Maggie noticed Cliff look at the tray.

'Why don't you have a coffee?' she suggested. 'It's bitter out there and it'll help warm you up.'

'Will you join me?'

Maggie hesitated, but Brian thrust two coffees down on the table and told them to help themselves to sugar and milk.

Maggie eased herself onto a wooden bench carefully so as not to spill the coffee. Cliff sat down opposite her, catching her eye as he did so.

'Is it still snowing?' she asked.

'Yes, and it's settling, but it's only a coating and will probably be gone by morning if we have the rain that's forecast.'

'It always looks so pretty,' said Maggie wistfully.

'Not much fun if you're sleeping out in it,' said Cliff, sipping his coffee.

'No,' agreed Maggie quickly. She felt herself blushing and told herself it was because she'd foolishly looked at the snow with romantic eyes instead of being practical and thinking how awful it would be to have to spend the night under a bridge or in a shop doorway, snow or no snow.

'In extremes of weather, the local

council and the Salvation Army come up with extra accommodation. They even help people who are not usually entitled to help, but only if the temperature drops below a certain point.'

'I'm very glad to hear it,' said Cliff.

'Have you got somewhere to sleep?' asked Maggie, battling with the image she had of Cliff, hair ruffled as he lay in a bed with crisp white sheets.

'Don't worry about me,' he was saying.

The hall was getting noisy. Most people had finished eating and were relaxing over a hot drink. Patrick was now playing requests, and some were singing along and clapping. It was a happy and almost carefree atmosphere, one that would be most welcome, even if it were only a short reprieve.

'In Dublin's fair city, where the girls are so pretty, I first set my eyes on sweet Molly Malone . . . '

Maggie looked up to find Cliff gazing at her with a strange look on his face. She thought it was because he was going to ask her something, but then he seemed to change his mind.

'Any more soup?' Brian asked as he gestured to a young couple who'd just arrived, covered in snow.

'Excuse me,' said Maggie as she took her coffee and left the table. 'Duty calls.'

She was disappointed that it hadn't been Jessica. Now she was doubting whether it had ever been her at all.

As soon as she'd served the young couple, she disappeared into a small storage room behind the kitchen. It was little more than a cupboard. There wasn't a lot of room, and it was full of boxes, but Maggie knew roughly what she was looking for.

'Need some help?' asked Cliff, his deep voice beginning to sound familiar but unnerving in an exciting sort of way.

Maggie spotted what she was looking for. 'There's a box of towels,' she explained. 'I just want two to offer to that pair who've just come in; they're drenched.'

'Here, let me,' offered Cliff as he reached

over to hold some boxes out of her way while Maggie pulled out two towels.

'Thank you,' she said. Briefly their hands touched as Cliff let the boxes fall back into place. He was now so close, she could smell his aftershave.

'You're absolutely wonderful,' breathed Cliff. 'I've never met anyone like you before.'

He towered above her but bent down and, placing his index finger under her chin, raised her face up to meet him. For a moment she thought he was going to kiss her. Her heart beat like a rhythmic drum-based backing theme to an unknown song.

They were still for what seemed like ages, but in reality it was only a few seconds. Cliff was looking at her and smiling. Maggie returned his smile and she searched for something to say. It was Cliff that broke the silence, and his words took her breath away.

'You're so special,' he told her in a hoarse whisper. 'I'm so glad I've found you.'

Maggie was not sure how to respond. Here she was in a tiny cupboard, surrounded by boxes of old clothes and bric-a-brac, being appraised by the most handsome man she had ever dreamed of, and yet she was cross with herself because she felt she sounded as though she'd been running a marathon and was all out of breath.

'Let me help you,' said Cliff, stepping back out of her way and holding her hand to steady her as she followed him, right into his arms, just for a second before he stepped back and released her. It had been enough, however, for her to realise that she would have liked a moment or two longer in his arms. She tried to put aside the thought and to think sensibly.

They paused for the briefest of moments, enough for Maggie to want to be taken into his arms and treasured, despite half of her brain telling her to be sensible. She wondered what Cliff was thinking.

A crash of crockery and a shout

disturbed them. Cliff took Maggie's hand, and together they returned to the hall, where a fight had broken out.

There was a lot of shouting and swearing. One man accused another of looking at him 'strangely'. He'd been drinking, and luckily when he swung his arm to hit the other chap, he completely missed, lost his balance and fallen onto one of the wooden tables. The legs collapsed and the dirty crockery crashed to the floor.

The drunken man lay on the floor, clutching his head. Someone suggested calling an ambulance, and instantly Brian was on his mobile.

Maggie could see it was all in hand, so she offered the towels to the young couple.

'Oh thanks,' said the girl as she wrapped the towel around herself like a blanket. Her lips were almost blue from the cold.

'Have you got somewhere to go tonight?' asked Maggie, and the girl nodded but was too wary to give away any details. Maggie smiled and left them to finish their soup. She got a tray and began to collect up the dirty bowls.

Within minutes, not only had an ambulance arrived but two police patrol cars. A moment later, the hall, which had been full of people happily singing away, was emptied, and only a handful of homeless people remained. Perhaps they had nothing to hide, or were too cold and hungry to move.

The paramedics checked the man. He was fine now and just wanted to curl up and sleep off his hangover.

The police questioned those who were still around. It wasn't aggressive questioning, just basic gathering of evidence should something more sinister develop. Maggie made more coffee and served all the officials.

'You won't believe it,' warned Brian. 'The story's grown from a drunk taking out his anger on the nearest person, to an organised raid with armed men.' Maggie laughed. 'Don't laugh,' he said. 'It'll be all over the newspapers tomorrow. It might even make the nationals.'

'Oh no,' groaned Maggie. If that were the case, her mother would be sure to read it and worry even more if she then found out about her daughter. 'Perhaps it won't come to that.'

A policeman approached. Maggie had been aware he'd been chatting with Cliff and now he was heading in her direction. She turned away to hide the smile that crept over her face. It had occurred to her that she might be asked what she was doing when the fight broke out. Could she really admit to being in a confined space with the gorgeous-looking Cliff?

'Thank you for the coffee,' said the policeman. 'Can I just ask you a few questions?'

Maggie answered his questions as best she could but felt she had very little to say.

'We don't usually have any trouble,' said Maggie again. 'He'd just had too much to drink. We don't serve any alcohol, so he must have been to the pub first.'

'No one is blaming you,' said the policeman, reassuring her. 'Is that what you're worried about?'

'Not me personally, but the church very kindly let us use their hall. If there's bad publicity, they may change their minds and throw us out.'

'Well, no one's been seriously hurt,' said the policeman.

'While you're here,' said Maggie, 'last Sunday our little wooden shed where we serve tea was burnt down. I don't suppose you have any information on that?'

'Did you report it?'

'I didn't, but one of the other volunteers did. There were no witnesses as far as I know, but it must have happened between about 12 noon and 4 p.m. The town's busy with shoppers at that time, and someone, perhaps from the multi-storey car park, might have seen something?'

Maggie knew she sounded too hopeful, but she could tell from the look the uniformed policeman gave her that they were never likely to know more about the burning of the tea bar.

'Why would anyone do that?' he asked, sounding genuinely puzzled.

'I suppose we attract what some residents may call 'undesirable' people to the area. I know there are one or two restaurants who would rather we didn't serve teas and encourage the homeless to wander about. But,' continued Maggie passionately, 'it's only for about an hour on a Sunday evening, no one lives close by, and we don't disturb anyone. We always clear up any rubbish before we go.'

'Isn't she wonderful when she's passionate?' Cliff said as he approached. He looked at the policeman and edged a little closer to Maggie as if to say, *Hands off, she's mine. I saw her first.*

A police radio crackled into life, and within moments they were gone, off to sort some other problem.

As they left, so too did the majority of the others, leaving just a small handful of volunteers to clear up, fill the dishwasher and lock up for the night.

Without being asked, Cliff helped to clear the tables. Maggie tidied up the kitchen while Brian and Cliff dismantled and folded away the tables. Another volunteer swept the hall, including the broken crockery.

It didn't take long to pack everything away. Cliff appeared at the kitchen hatch.

'I wondered if I could walk you home?' he asked.

Maggie felt torn. She longed to spend more time with this man, but she knew nothing about him, and knew she must not mix business with pleasure. George the church warden came to her rescue.

'Before you go, Maggie, I've got some papers I need you to take over to your father. They're in my office, if I can find them.'

'Thanks for the offer,' said Maggie to Cliff. 'Maybe another time?'

'See you again then,' said Cliff as he headed off toward the heavy wooden door with George following him, ready with his keys.

'What papers?' asked Maggie a few minutes later.

'There are no papers, but I've noticed that young man keeps looking at you, and you can never be too sure,' warned George.

Brian was emptying the bins; he looked up and nodded. 'I'd also noticed him watching you — not in a nasty way, but he obviously fancies you.'

'Oh,' said Maggie, feeling delighted, but knowing she ought to be wary.

'I did take the liberty of asking around to find out more about him, but no one knows him at all. I don't think he's sleeping rough, by the looks of him, and no one recognised him from the hostels,' said Brian.

'I wondered if he was a policeman or maybe a social worker,' suggested Maggie.

'He could be, but if he was, he didn't own up to the police today. I was standing right near him when they interviewed him about tonight, and he hardly gave anything away. He's Cliff Hunter, by the way, and lives in Blackthorn Road, I think he said.'

'Never heard of it,' said George.

'He's not tagged,' remarked Brian in a matter-of-fact way as though he always looked at people's ankles to see if they wore a police tag.

'Well, thank goodness for that,' said Maggie. She'd never even given it a thought, and yet she knew she ought to be more professional. He could be a drug dealer or common thief. What would her mother say to that? she wondered.

'He did have big feet,' continued Brian. 'Could be undercover police. Maybe he's with the drug squad?'

'Well, we may have seen the last of him,' said Maggie, briskly trying to move the conversation on. 'How was the man who bumped his head?'

'He was fine, but the ambulance men took him just to check him out because he had banged his head and they wanted to make sure he wasn't concussed. I'm sure he'll be fine. He was able to give his name, and was even joking about how the National Health Service would provide him with free bed and breakfast accommodation for the night. At least that will be better than a police cell.'

'You're not walking home in this tonight, are you?' George asked Maggie.

'I've got the car,' she reassured him.

'Perhaps I should follow you home,' said Brian. 'I wouldn't want him to stalk you.'

'I really didn't feel threatened by him, or anyone,' said Maggie quickly.

'I'd agree, he seemed polite and helpful. I had a chat with him about the new shopping centre and gallery.' George gave a knowing look in Maggie's direction. 'I just wanted to check him out. We can't have anything happening to you, Maggie!'

'Nothing's going to happen to me,' she said decisively. 'Although I shall be in big trouble with my mum if a story is printed about drug users and guns in a local church hall while volunteers serve soup. She'll never understand what it's really like.'

'Have you told her, then?' Brian asked.

'No, not yet,' Maggie admitted. 'But I will. I've just got to find the right moment, and things keep getting in my way.'

'I can't see your dad being too happy you being here if he thought you were in danger,' said George, who'd known Rev Robert Brown for many years.

'Thank you both for being so concerned for my well-being,' said Maggie firmly, 'but I'm sure you really haven't got anything to worry about.' She took a deep breath and said, 'He'll probably move on and we'll never see him again.'

George and Brian looked at each other and smiled.

'I'm not a betting man,' said Brian, 'but I'd put money on that he'll be there on Sunday when you serve the teas.'

Maggie took off her apron and rolled it up to take home and wash. She tried to distance herself from the conversation. Sunday was five days away, and it was going to seem like a lifetime waiting for it to come around just so she could catch a glimpse of this relative stranger, although she had an advantage on him. She now knew his full name and part of his address, so perhaps she'd spend a bit of time between now and Sunday doing some detective work of her own.

3

Maggie's plans for detective work were completely thrown by her mother's plans to hold a charity dinner at the weekend.

She had already agreed to do the flowers for the hall and dining room, but her mother had several more 'little jobs' for her daughter to be involved with.

'You've done a fantastic job,' Robert said to his wife as he was invited to do a tour of the house before the first guest arrived.

'I couldn't have done it without Margaret, she's been a star!'

Maggie knew she was supposed to be chatting to the special guests and dignitaries, but that really didn't make her feel comfortable. She was much happier serving the dainty pastries and topping up sherry glasses. She always felt better when she was busy doing something practical.

This evening seemed in such complete contrast to the rest of her life. Here she was in a full-length bronze-coloured evening dress that her mother had given her for Christmas. It was a simple enough design, but it was a couture gown, and the perfect colour for her long brown curly hair. This evening she wore her hair up in a twisted knot at the back of her head. Her necklace and earrings were Goldstone, which sparkled but didn't dazzle. She wore dainty bronze ballet-style shoes that complemented her outfit. Her mother had tried to persuade her to wear high heels, but Maggie knew she'd totter around all evening and regret it in the morning when her feet were sore and her back ached.

'You're too old for your years,' her mother had remarked. 'I loved pretty high heels when I was your age.'

'They do look nice, but they really aren't very comfortable, and I'm walking the dog with Angela in the morning, so I don't want to be hobbling around all night in shoes I can't walk in.'

She would have to admit she enjoyed dressing up some times, but was equally comfortable in her practical and warm clothes when she worked at the tea bar, or her jeans and jumper when she visited some of her father's parishioners in hospital or in the local retirement home.

'And here's my daughter, Margaret,' said Nancy Haddon-Brown.

'I think we've already met,' said the tall, clean-shaven blue-eyed man with a gleam in his eyes. Cliff looked very different in his crisp white shirt and black tie, his stubbly beard gone and his hair neatly brushed.

'No, I don't think so,' said Maggie quickly. 'I'm Margaret,' she emphasised as she offered him her hand. She pleaded with her eyes that he would not give her double life away.

Cliff seemed amused by this, as if he

now had some hold over her. 'It'll cost you,' he whispered while Nancy's attention was diverted by another guest.

Maggie looked at him, trying to decide what he meant.

'I'd settle for a kiss,' he whispered into her ear, his breath hot on her skin. It was like a touch paper lighting and spreading a fire of desire through her body. But Maggie was just thankful that he didn't let on.

'Margaret's done all the beautiful flowers,' continued Nancy. 'She's done a floristry course and is thinking of setting up her own business in the village.'

'Is she really?' said Cliff with a smile. 'She's certainly got a flair for colour. That's the perfect dress for you.'

'Are you still going to that conference next week?' Nancy asked her daughter, obviously trying to draw her into the conversation with the intention of getting Maggie to talk with Cliff.

'The small business one at the Thorns Hotel?' asked Maggie.

'Yes,' said her mother, encouraging her to put down the tray of sherry glasses and engage this handsome young man in conversation. 'You were working on a business plan to take with you.'

'Yes I was, but I haven't finished it yet. I really am in two minds about wanting my own shop,' confessed Maggie, 'although I do want to be independent.'

'But I thought that was why you did the course, dear.'

'I did the course to learn how to arrange flowers. It's very therapeutic. I'd love to work with flowers, but not necessarily owning and running a florist's.'

'The small business conference may be just what you need to help you make up your mind about what you do want,' suggested Cliff.

'What a sensible young man,' said Nancy as she filled up his glass.

Discreetly, one of the waiting staff came and whispered in Maggie's ear that she was wanted on the phone.

'Excuse me a moment,' she said, ignoring her mother's frown.

Nancy leaned a bit closer to Cliff and took his arm, steering him toward the large open fireplace.

'Actually,' she said as though she were now able to confide in Cliff, 'I'm a bit worried about Margaret. She won't tell me, but I think she's seeing a young man.' Nancy laughed lightly.

'Well she's a very attractive woman,' said Cliff. 'I'm not at all surprised she's sought after.'

'She thinks I don't notice her slipping out every Sunday evening and on Tuesdays. Of course she could be going to evensong with her father, but just recently she's come home with such a spring in her step and a sort of glow. I'm a woman, and I know when a girl's in love.' Nancy paused. 'You did say you'd met her before?'

'I think I must have been mistaken. I think she reminds me of someone, that's all.'

Cliff finished his drink and glanced toward the door where Maggie had just reentered. The clock on the mantelpiece struck eight, rather like a dinner gong. This was the cue for Nancy to gently guide her guests into the large dining room.

'Important call?' Cliff asked as he found himself walking into the dining room beside Maggie.

'I had some flowers left over, so I made a table decoration and took it over to my friend, Angela. She's been feeling a bit down lately, but she was out, and had only just got home, and wanted to thank me. She looks after her elderly father, and he's getting more and more frail, and it upsets her,' Maggie told him politely, although she wondered why he was asking. It wasn't really any of his business, but she had been brought up not to be rude to guests. Perhaps he was just making small talk as they walked into dinner, she told herself.

'Quite the little saint,' said Cliff in a teasing voice.

'I try to be good and serve others,' said Maggie seriously. Instantly a collage of thoughts muddled her mind.

She was guilty of not being open and honest with her own mother. She felt guilty for living such a privileged life at Haddon Hall when others around her had very little. She knew she liked this man a lot more than she felt she ought to; he was little more than a stranger, after all. In fact, thought Maggie, she'd believed he was homeless and now realised he certainly wasn't penniless and desperate.

'Now you sit there, Mr Hunter,' said Nancy. 'And Margaret, you go over there between Mr Smith and Mr Bertram.'

Maggie found herself opposite Cliff, with two middle-aged gentlemen on each side of her, while Cliff sat on the opposite side of the table with a stunning blonde model on his left, and a dazzlingly attractive young woman on his right side.

All of a sudden Maggie wanted the evening to be over so she could curl up in bed and dream her safe dreams instead of having to sit opposite this man who was causing her sleepless nights.

The model was introducing herself to Cliff, obviously not wanting to waste any time at all. As she offered him her hand, Maggie noticed the long red talons and the huge diamond ring with matching bracelet, necklace and ear-rings. The blonde was dripping with money and openly making eyes at Cliff.

It wasn't nice to watch, thought Maggie, but what surprised her was that she felt jealous. She felt she had some right to Cliff because she had met him before, or maybe because he shared her secret. The blonde began to paw at Cliff's arm, as he'd turned away from her and smiled at Maggie.

Cliff had still not taken the woman's hand in her offered handshake. Maggie wanted to smile as she watched Cliff briefly shake the woman's hand before immediately turning away from her to the woman on his other side. He then moved his chair back a little so the two women could introduce themselves and carry on their conversation.

Maggie's eyes met Cliff's. She thought

she saw a kindred spirit. Perhaps it was just wishful thinking. It looked like he was someone who also wanted to escape, but who knew they had a duty to perform.

Maggie's mother always put on an excellent dinner party. Hours of planning would have gone into this; not that Nancy had done much of the actual cooking. Maggie was determined to interrogate her mother for any morsel of information on Cliff Hunter. She was hungry to find out more about him — or was it she was just hungry for Cliff himself?

'That was delicious,' said the gentleman beside Maggie.

'All locally produced food,' Maggie explained. 'My mother likes to support local businesses.'

'As we all do,' said Mr Smith. 'I hear you may be buying the old chemist's in the village, now they've moved up the high street?'

'I did look at it with a view to opening a florist's, but I think it's too big for what I need.'

'What about the newsagent's at the other end of the High Street?' he asked.

'That would probably be a better size, but I'm not really sure I want a shop.'

Once again Maggie glanced up and caught Cliff looking in her direction. He was leaning back, having finished his meal.

Maggie sipped her wine and wondered whether she ought to organise a working party to clear away the burnt-out tea bar.

'I'm sorry,' she said a moment later when her mother asked her something, 'I was miles away.'

'I wondered if you'd like to take some of our guests into the lounge for coffee,' repeated Nancy. This had already been agreed and planned beforehand, but right now there was only one guest Maggie wanted to take into the lounge, though she guessed they would not be alone for long.

'Of course,' said Maggie, pushing her

chair back and shaking her linen napkin before putting it carefully down on the table. 'Coffee?' she asked generally, but looking at Cliff. He took the cue and stood to leave the table.

'So, what are you doing here?' asked Maggie as she poured the coffee for a handful of guests in the lounge.

'I was invited,' said Cliff simply.

'But why?' pressed Maggie, aware that she sounded a bit abrupt.

'I could say I'd hoped you'd added me to the list, but I think you were as surprised as I was to find you here.'

'I'll check the guest list in the morning to make sure you haven't been gate-crashing,' teased Maggie. 'Although my mother does have discreet security men around on these occasions.'

'I have to say you do spruce up quite well,' said Cliff, looking at her appreciably.

'Thank you,' said Maggie. 'You've cleaned up well yourself. And to think you said you were homeless!'

'I never said I was homeless. You just

made an assumption.'

'I . . . ' began Maggie, but they were joined by another couple. 'Can I pour you some coffee?' she asked sweetly.

The room was filling up quickly. The guests who'd waited in the dining room with Maggie's parents to enjoy a liqueur with their coffee were now filtering through into the lounge. Despite it being winter and the fire dying in the grate, the room was warm, and Maggie's dad was opening the French windows onto the patio. As if by magic, lights came on and lit up the carefully manicured gardens.

The evening had all been in aid of raising money to buy a small plot of land at the far end of town. There was a new estate. The houses were neat and modern with gardens only big enough to house a barbecue. There was nowhere for children to play, and the local primary school was overcrowded due to all the new houses, and had been forced to build on their playing field. There had been an outcry at the time, but no one had come up with an alternative, so the building had gone ahead. Then a fire had burnt down an old hotel and it had been demolished.

'Feel free to have a good look at the plans to build a children's playground on the site of the Old Bell Hotel,' said Nancy Haddon-Brown. 'Nothing's set in stone, so if you have a suggestion, do let me know. Obviously the local council will have to approve any ideas we have.'

The guests politely showed interest in the plans and one or two immediately pledged money, much to Nancy's delight.

'Looking at this house and grounds,' said one man, 'it appears as though your mother could just buy a playground all by herself.'

'That was what my great-grandfather would have done. You must have seen some of the things he's left — Haddon Garage, Haddon Road, Haddon memorial ground, near the church?' Nancy explained.

'Of course.' The man nodded.

'My mother wants to get the rest of the village involved so that everyone feels part of it, and feels they've helped the local school and the children that live in the new estate,' Maggie added.

She sat down on the leather Chesterfield settee beside the trolley with the coffee. Cliff immediately came over to join her, sitting close and draping his arm across the back of the low sofa, protectively around Maggie's back, but not actually touching her. Despite this, Maggie was all too aware of his closeness. She had never felt so charged with excitement.

'And of course,' added Cliff, 'a property like this and the grounds cost a great deal of upkeep. It may seem like a wonderful place to own, but big old houses like these can be a huge drain on resources.'

'They certainly are,' echoed Robert. He was dressed in black with his white dog collar, as he represented the local church as well as being their host.

'Dad!' said Maggie excitedly. 'May I introduce you to Mr Hunter?'

Cliff stood and held out his hand. 'Pleased to meet you, sir.'

'And you, Mr Hunter.' Robert smiled. 'I daresay you know all about old houses with your connection with Blackthorn Manor.'

Maggie noted 'Blackthorn Manor' and not 'Blackthorn Road', as she'd originally been told when she'd made her initial enquiries.

'I do. It's not just the buildings themselves, but the regulations about what you can and cannot do.'

'I had a great battle some years ago when I first married,' began Robert, engaging Cliff in conversation so Maggie could sit back and watch these two special men chat to each other in a relaxed and natural way. 'Nancy had this place, so we really didn't need to live in the vicarage. But when I proposed to convert the vicarage into cheap accommodation for local youngsters so they could live independently in the village, while saving up for a deposit on their own place, there was a great uproar.'

'But you got there in the end,' said Nancy as she offered round an enormous box of chocolates for people to enjoy with their coffee. 'No one likes change, but you had the whole village on your side in the end. It's wonderful how many young couples you've helped get on the property market who have all been married in All Saints, and now we're busy christening their children.'

'It's what a community is all about,' said Robert.

Maggie had heard all this before, many a time, but now she seemed to listen it with new ears. All her senses, it seemed, were on red alert as she became aware of each word, each individual aroma. She could smell the embers of the fire, which reminded her of the burnt-out tea bar. She could smell her mother's expensive perfume and the soap her father always used. But the strongest aroma was of Cliff's aftershave. She'd first noticed it the other evening when he'd helped her in the storage cupboard. The thought made her want to laugh out loud, but somehow she managed to control herself. She was sure she could smell his distinctive aftershave now. It seemed to be on her shoulder, where she'd been sitting next to him and where, earlier on in the evening, he'd whispered to her.

The group began to break up as the some of the guests made their donations to the children's park and fetched their coats ready to go. Cliff discreetly handed Nancy his donation. Maggie had hardly noticed, but she had seen the surprised look on her mother's face.

'That's very generous, Mr Hunter,' she said.

'I used to go to school there, and I loved climbing the trees at playtimes and kicking a stone around with my friends. I'm lucky to be able to give something back.'

'Well, that's very kind of you, and I'll make sure you're invited to the opening when we've bought the land and got planning permission.'

'Thank you,' said Cliff, and looking at Maggie, he continued, 'I'd like you to keep in touch.'

The look was not lost on Nancy, who instantly stood and nodded to her husband to move away.

'Please excuse me while I see to my other guests,' she said, and steered the Rev. Robert Brown away, leaving Cliff and Maggie alone together.

'I ought to go too, I suppose,' said Cliff as the guests were thinning out and the room began to cool down. Robert closed the French windows and poked the fire.

'Thanks for . . . ' began Maggie, looking in the direction of her mother.

'No problem.' He winked. 'But you do owe me.'

Maggie gave him a look.

'I think I deserve at least one kiss,' he said, keeping his voice low.

Maggie stood, putting on an act of pretending she had not heard what he'd said, and collected up a few coffee cups. Cliff stood too, and held out his hand as he walked toward the lounge door which led back into the hall where he had left his coat. She watched as he put on his coat and scarf, and thought again how handsome he was.

'Goodnight,' he said formally to Nancy and Robert, and then turned to Maggie, who lent forward, standing on tiptoes so she could reach to plant a kiss on his cheek.

'Now we're equal,' she whispered. Then in her normal voice she said, 'Thank you so much for coming.'

'It's been a pleasure, believe me,' said Cliff with a knowing smile.

Maggie walked with Cliff to the front door. She shivered.

'Don't get cold. You wait indoors. My taxi will be here any minute.' Gently Cliff pushed her back inside, giving her arm the gentlest of squeezes as he did so. It seemed to say such a lot.

Maggie went inside and made her way to the lounge window, which looked out onto the front. A black taxi had just arrived. Maggie watched as Cliff headed for it, pulling his coat collar around him to keep out the cold night air.

Just as he reached the car, he looked back. He noticed Maggie at the lounge window, waved, and then blew her a kiss.

She smiled as she caught it and went to bed with happy thoughts.

4

Maggie arrived at the conference room in the hotel in her smart black pin-striped business suit. She bent down to sign in at a table near the doorway when a deep voice interrupted her.

'Good morning,' Cliff said. 'Are you Maggie or Margaret today?'

Maggie felt a shot of electricity run through her body. Her mind had been full of Cliff ever since he had blown her that kiss on Saturday evening, right through to waking up his morning with his name on her lips.

He'd not been at the tea bar on Sunday evening, and Maggie had missed him. She'd even worried if he was all right and had wondered about trying to contact him, but of course there was no reason for him to be there, and she had talked herself out of it.

'I'm Maggie. In fact I'm always Maggie,' she said rather crossly. 'It's only my mother who insists on calling me Margaret, but then I suppose she chose my name in the first place.'

She was annoyed with herself for snapping at the very man she was longing to see, and didn't wait while he signed in. However, Cliff was obviously not that easily put off and followed her to the refreshment table, where there was an extensive range of teas and coffees.

'We always seem to meet round coffee bars,' said Cliff.

'I missed you on Sunday,' said Maggie quietly. 'I was hoping . . . ' She stumbled on her words and then corrected herself. 'I was expecting to see you.'

'I had business of my own to attend to,' said Cliff mysteriously. He was watching her, staring at her intently.

'What's wrong?' asked Maggie after a moment or two of feeling as though he were actually undressing her.

'There's absolutely nothing wrong!' said Cliff with a smile. 'It's just that now I've seen you in your casual jeans and jumper, your elegant evening dress and now a business suit, and I was wondering which I like best.'

Part of Maggie thought it was none of his business what she wore or even that he should have an opinion about what she may or may not look like, but she was also intrigued, and it got the better of her.

'OK,' she said in a tired voice as though she wasn't really interested, 'so, which do you like best?'

'I think I'd still like to see one or two more options,' he said with a cheeky grin. Maggie gave him a mocked disapproving look. He said seriously, 'In that case, I thought you looked absolutely beautiful in your evening gown, but far more comfortable in your jeans. Even though that suit shows all your curves, it's not you.'

'Oh,' said Maggie in surprise. She'd never had such an open and honest appraisal of herself before. 'Perhaps next time I go shopping, I'll forget my girlfriends and ask you to come and help me choose an outfit!'

'I hate shopping!' confessed Cliff. 'I suppose I just like looking.'

Maggie gave him another of her disapproving looks and found herself a table near the front but to the left-hand side. She wanted to be able to hear and see all without being stuck right in the middle. Cliff joined her.

'Did you get out of bed on the wrong side this morning?' he asked.

'Whatever makes you ask that?' she snapped again without meaning to. 'I'm sorry,' she said quickly. 'I don't know what's wrong with me this morning.'

'Would you rather I moved away?' asked Cliff, looking at her very seriously with his twinkling blue eyes.

Maggie had just been wondering how she was ever going to concentrate with him sitting so close to her, but really, the fact that he was in the same room was going to be enough to put her off the business of the day.

'No, that's fine, and I promise I'll try to be civil.'

'Is it so hard?'

'Of course not!' she snapped again. 'It's just that you have this strange effect on me.'

'Oh,' he said seriously. 'It's all my fault, is it?'

Maggie was about to correct herself when she saw the corners of his mouth turn up, and he gave her the most heart-warming grin she thought she had ever seen. He not only smiled with his mouth, but with his eyes. In fact his whole face lit up. Maggie couldn't help but return his smile.

'Yes,' she said decisively, 'it is your fault.'

Cliff's smile changed to an inquiring look and Maggie went weak at the knees. She was close to confessing that she'd been thinking of nothing but him night and day and was desperate to see him again. It all so nearly came spilling out of Maggie's unchecked mouth that she was relieved when the course leader coughed to announce he was about to start talking. She knew she had probably said too much about the way Cliff made her feel and react. It was as if she were no longer in control of her own body. It had already surrendered itself to him.

The conference facilitator introduced himself and gave a brief summary of the course. He then asked if everyone would introduce themselves, and say what they did, and why they were here. He looked straight at Maggie to start them off.

'I'm Maggie Brown,' she began. 'I've done a floristry course and I'm wondering how I can use it in the world of business. I don't think I want to go down the route of a high street shop, although I do like the idea of working with people. I'm hoping today will help me make up my mind what I want to do.'

The facilitator nodded encouragingly and then looked at Cliff sitting beside her.

'I'm Cliff Hunter, and I want to help

a group of men who are trying to give up drugs. I want them to be able to set up their own small businesses so they can learn new skills and get work experience in a safe environment. Eventually, I'll want to equip them with the skills to move on and get a real job, once they're free of the drugs.'

It took some time for everyone to introduce themselves, and then they watched a slide show presentation.

It was soon time for a coffee break. 'Still cross with me?' Cliff asked.

'You pretended you were homeless!' exclaimed Maggie, not wanting to let on that she was pleased that he wasn't.

'I must apologise if you thought that, but many of the people I work with have been homeless, and I just wanted to try and understand what it feels like, and what sort of problems they might face. It was really good to see what's on offer locally.'

'Oh,' said Maggie as she realised that would be exactly what she would do. She had not met many men who were so ready to empathize with the people they worked with. Despite herself, she was beginning to have more and more respect for this unwelcome intruder in her life.

'Besides,' continued Cliff, 'I didn't pretend to be homeless. I was just there, and it was you who made the assumption.'

Maggie looked down at her feet, knowing that what he said was true. She *had* assumed he was homeless.

'Shall I get you a coffee, for a change?' he asked. 'Maybe then you'll begin to forgive me?'

'Thank you,' said Maggie. 'Black coffee, no sugar.'

Cliff was back very quickly with two coffees. 'Actually, I'm glad we've got this opportunity to spend the day together,' he said. 'Maybe we can start afresh and get to know each other a bit better?'

Maggie could not help wondering if all her mother's hints had rubbed off on him and that was really why he was here. Perhaps she did have something to thank her mother for, after all.

'I wondered if you fancied going for a meal tonight after the course?'

'I couldn't possibly go out with a complete stranger!' said Maggie, but with a smile on her face.

'We've met on several occasions now,' Cliff reminded her, and just to show he was serious, he added, 'So, do you like Chinese food or Indian food? Or Italian, or what?'

'They all sound good, but lunch is included in today's course, so I doubt if I'll be able to eat another meal tonight.'

'Nonsense!' said Cliff. 'We'll only get a few sandwiches at lunchtime. You'll be starving by this evening.'

'I have to watch my figure, you know,' teased Maggie.

'Don't worry about that. It'll be all my pleasure to watch your figure for you,' said Cliff. His face broke into a broad grin again, and everything inside Maggie just seemed to melt away.

It took her some time to focus in on

what was actually being said by the man who was leading the course. She often found she had switched off and was busy studying Cliff's strong hands or his side profile. Occasionally she caught him looking at her. Then, she'd quickly look away and pretend to study her notes.

The morning flew past. Cliff steered Maggie out towards the dining room when it was time for lunch.

'Excuse me, Mr Hunter,' said the facilitator. 'I was interested to hear what you had to say about your project.'

'Good,' said Cliff, who once again gently touched Maggie's arm as if to lead her out of the conference room and towards the dining room. He was obviously hungry for lunch, thought Maggie.

'If I were you,' continued the facilitator, following along with them, 'I would forget the homeless people. You own Blackthorn Manor. I've read all about you in the newspaper. You'd be so much better to sell the land to a developer and build a housing estate on it. You could make a pretty penny!'

Until this point Maggie, had quietly gone happily along toward the dining room, glad to have Cliff by her side, but this was too much. She could not keep her mouth closed.

'Don't you dare!' she said with feeling to Cliff. 'What would the drug addicts do if people like you sold up and made money from houses instead of investing in people like them, who only have a future because of you? You could give so much hope to them. You could literally save their lives!'

'Don't worry, Maggie,' said Cliff. 'I've no intention of selling up. Although if I did, I might have more money to be able to invest, and maybe that would be better in the long run. Then I could use the money to build a purpose-built hostel and maybe even give the men a grant to get them started.'

'You'd be foolish to give a drug addict any money,' said Maggie seriously. 'The chances are that they'd just spend it on drugs and they'd be worse off, rather than better.'

Cliff laughed loudly as he listened to Maggie's passionate speech and then served himself to a generous helping of the hot buffet meal provided. It wasn't just sandwiches after all.

'So you're not so innocent and gullible after all!' he chuckled.

'I'm not stupid, if that's what you mean,' said Maggie defensively.

'I never, ever thought you were stupid, but I admit I did wonder if you were too nice to really know what happens in the real world.'

'I'm not that naive,' said Maggie.

'Obviously not.' Cliff put his plate down on a table for two and gestured that Maggie should do the same. The course facilitator stood with his plate. He hesitated for a moment and then went, somewhat reluctantly, to join another delegate's table.

They ate their dinner in silence for the first few minutes.

'Is there any reason you're only planning on helping male drug addicts?' asked Maggie after a while.

'Not really. All of my contacts so far happen to be male, and it makes accommodation easier if I just have men; but I do have a wing that's not being used, and that could be for women. I thought I might split up the younger men from the older ones, but I don't need to do that.'

'How far ahead is your plan?' asked Maggie.

'Actually, it's mainly in my head at the moment. I have had plans drawn up, but I only inherited the property a year ago, and it's in a bad state. I really ought to get started on this project before the place actually starts falling down.'

'It can't be that bad!' laughed Maggie.

'You should see where I live. In fact, you'd be most welcome to come and see it, and the plans, of course,' he added. 'I may not actually be homeless, but the plaster's crumbling and there's some dry rot and draughty window frames.'

'Are you trying to make me feel sorry for you?'

81

'I was hoping you'd offer to come and keep me warm,' retorted Cliff with a smile. 'You can't blame me for trying!'

* * *

The afternoon was spent making their own business plans with a view to approaching a bank for a business loan. One by one they were invited to give a presentation of their business idea to a panel, rather like *Dragon's Den*.

'I don't need a loan,' Maggie told Cliff, 'and I don't particularly need to make a profit. I suppose I ought to cover my costs, but I'd much rather do something useful. I did wonder about doing more training so I could teach floristry at college, or even in the special school at Uphill.'

'Or to inmates at my drug rehabilitation unit?' asked Cliff.

'I'm not qualified yet,' said Maggie but his idea had appealed to her more than anything else she had thought of in a long time. This was actually something she could see herself doing. She would love to work with the flowers, and it would satisfy her if she could share that enjoyment with others. And if they went on to get a proper job and kick the drug habit, then that would definitely tick all her boxes. It would even give her the perfect excuse to see more of Cliff, and that was exciting in itself.

Maggie politely listened while one after another, people gave their presentations, but they were of no real interest to her. After the second one, she found herself daydreaming. Suddenly she was back in Cliff's arms just as she had been in the store cupboard. She could feel the warmth from his masculine body next to hers. She could smell his aftershave and even feel how much he desired her.

'Miss Brown?' said a voice out of the blue. 'It's your turn.'

'Actually, I've decided I need to enrol for some more training,' said Maggie. 'I won't take up any more of your time right now.'

'What sort of additional training?' asked the facilitator, not letting her get away with things too easily.

'Possibly teacher training.'

'For adults or children?'

'Is it different training?' asked Maggie.

'Very different. I have some leaflets, if that would be useful.'

'Thank you.'

At the end of the course, Maggie filled in her evaluation form with a positive mind. She now had a much clearer idea of what she wanted to do. She was going to approach the local college to see if she could train to teach adults in floristry and ideally work with different groups of adults to teach them flower arranging. She would be delighted to work with Cliff's drug addicts, if any of them were interested. She would see it as a sort of art therapy. She'd also apply to the local special school to see if she could do some work experience.

After a while, Maggie became aware

that Cliff was standing over her, waiting for her to finish filling in her form.

'I'm not letting you go until I have a definite date to see you again,' he said. 'In fact, I don't even have your phone number, although I suppose I know where you live now.'

'You also know where I'll be on a Sunday and a Tuesday evening,' Maggie reminded him.

'I was hoping to have you to myself,' said Cliff, moving a little closer to her. 'Come and have dinner with me tonight?' he asked again.

'I'm just not hungry,' said Maggie, who'd completely lost her appetite. 'But we could have a drink in the bar,' she suggested, as she didn't want to let him go either.

'Deal,' said Cliff quickly.

They were just leaving the conference suite when the facilitator approached them again. 'Mr Hunter,' he called. Cliff looked round. 'I wonder, can I just have a little word?'

'Is it important?' asked Cliff, holding

on to Maggie's hand so that she wouldn't disappear.

'It will certainly be worth your while,' he continued. 'Just a quick word in private, if I may?' The last phrase was directed at Maggie.

Cliff squeezed her hand. 'You can say anything in front of my business partner.'

'Oh, I didn't realise you were in this together.'

He continued to make Cliff another even more generous offer for the land that Blackthorn Manor stood on. He knew builders and had contacts and was ready to do a deal here and now.

'Thank you,' said Cliff politely as he took the letter with the offer written on it. 'I'm sure you'll appreciate it's a big decision, and I need to give it some thought.'

'My number's on there when you're ready to give me a ring.' He offered his hand to Cliff.

'Thank you for the course today,' said Cliff, shaking his hand.

Just as they did, someone took a photo of the two of them shaking hands as if they had agreed upon a deal.

'You're not seriously going to consider that offer, are you?' said Maggie when they were alone in the bar.

'I'd be a fool not to consider it, but I have no plans to sell up for housing, or for anything else for that matter.'

'Promise?'

'No, I won't promise. You'll have to trust that my intentions are honourable.'

'I don't trust him.'

'You don't know him. He's just trying to make a living, like many other people.'

'But that's exactly it!' Maggie exclaimed. 'He's only interested in the money, not the people.'

'I suspect you're right, but you're only interested in the people, and in business I think you need to keep an open mind and consider all the options until you make a decision.'

In many ways Maggie knew what he said was correct, but in her heart she still didn't trust anyone who seemed to just see pound signs.

'Now, what can I get you to drink?' asked Cliff.

5

Maggie finished her coffee.

'Are you sure you won't have another coffee, or something stronger?' asked Cliff.

'I suppose I ought to be getting home,' Maggie replied, looking at her empty cup.

'But the night is yet young! If you won't let me buy you dinner, at least have another drink with me?'

'Okay,' agreed Maggie. 'But I must give my parents a ring and just let them know I'm all right and I won't need tea.'

While Cliff went off to get two more coffees, Maggie tried to get a signal on her phone.

'Hi, Mum,' she said at last. 'I'll be home a bit later.'

'Was the course useful?' asked Nancy.

'Yes,' said Maggie, and before she

knew it she said, 'You'll never guess who was here today. Cliff Hunter — you remember, from the fund-raising evening?'

'I do remember him. Fancy you two meeting up again so soon.' Maggie could hear the smile in her mother's voice.

'Well you did tell him I'd be here. We're just having a drink and then I'll be home.'

'No rush,' said Nancy. 'Your father's busy in his study, and I've got a committee meeting tonight, so we probably wouldn't see you until the morning. If you're hungry when you get home, there's some cold meat and salad in the fridge.' She paused. 'There's enough for two, if you wanted to bring a friend home.'

'Thanks,' said Maggie, ignoring her mother's invitation. 'See you later.'

She returned to the bar. A large cup of coffee was waiting for her.

'Did you get hold of your parents?' asked Cliff. Maggie nodded. 'Why don't you tell them the truth?'

'The truth?' asked Maggie, sounding shocked. She hadn't lied to them about where she was and she resented him assuming that she had.

'Are you ashamed?' continued Cliff.

'Ashamed? What, of being here with you?'

'You know that's not what I meant,' said Cliff with a sigh. 'I hope you're not ashamed to be here with me. I meant ashamed of your charity work.'

'My father knows. In fact, he was the one who got me interested.'

'I suppose you'll say it's all his fault,' teased Cliff, but Maggie was beginning to feel on edge.

'It was my father's fault,' said Maggie. 'But there's a good reason I haven't yet got around to mentioning it to my mother. She worries, and she'd be horrified if she knew what I was actually doing.'

'So, are you ashamed?'

'No, definitely not. But I want to protect her and, if I'm honest, I don't want her to be constantly nagging at me to be careful, and to take this precaution or that.'

'Your mother struck me as the sort of person who'd approve of your good works,' said Cliff.

'You don't know my mother. You've only met her once, and she was on her best behaviour then,' snapped Maggie.

'OK, so tell me about your mother,' said Cliff as he put down his coffee cup and sat back ready to listen.

'Well she's a worrier.'

'You've already told me that,' said Cliff, not making it easy for her. 'I bet the majority of mothers worry about their children. I'm sure I would if I had a daughter.'

Maggie was completely thrown for a moment. The thought of Cliff with a daughter conjured up a wonderful warm glow inside her. She could see he'd make a natural family man. He was just the sort of man she would choose to father her children, if she were ever to want a family. Up until now, she had never really given it much thought.

She became aware that Cliff was looking at her again. He was obviously waiting for her to speak.

'Mum worries about everything. That's why I rang her to tell her where I was. She worries if I'm just five minutes late; or if she hears of any accident on the road, she phones me just to check I'm OK.'

'There's nothing really wrong with that. In fact, I think it's wonderful that she cares so much about you.'

'My mother reads a lot. She keeps up with all the news and what's going on in the world. She often comments on the homeless and in particular about drug users. She's made comments about how violent the drugs can make people, and how when they share needles, they might get AIDS and die. I think she did some hospital visits some years ago on a ward with young men dying from AIDS, mainly due to drug-related problems. Then all at once things started happening, and I think a member of the hospital staff was caught selling drugs and suspended. Then two or maybe three of the patients died, and that really upset her. And then, to top it all, she was visiting one day when the police did a drugs raid on the hospital ward because they thought more staff were involved in supplying drugs, and she was caught up in it all. The whole experience has tarnished what she feels.'

'Well, you can understand where she's coming from,' said Cliff.

'Don't you sympathise with her!' said Maggie. 'That was one relatively small incident about ten years ago.'

'But it obviously had a big effect on her. Surely you can see that.'

'I *can* see, but she always seems to forget all the drug users who are weaned off their drugs and make a clean go of it in society.'

'Are there many stories with happy endings?' asked Cliff.

'Oh yes,' assured Maggie. 'Although I

suppose they're outweighed by the tragic ones, and those make the newspapers. But there are success stories too, believe me.'

'I have to believe you, and you might need to share them with me if, or when, things get tough with the group of people I'm working with.'

'Are they just from the hospital?' asked Maggie.

'There's a drug rehabilitation clinic which is under threat of being closed purely for financial reasons. The trustees aren't very sympathetic. They see drug abuse as self-inflicted, which I suppose it is really, although many are led into it. Anyway, the trustees would rather put their money and resources into something that helps people with illnesses and diseases that they can't do anything about. Although I can see their point — where does it leave those poor kids who are trying to wean themselves off drugs and need all the support they can get?'

'It's not just me who can talk

passionately about something,' said Maggie with a wry smile.

'Perhaps that's what you should do with your mother. Show her how much you care and why you give up your time, and that will win her over.'

'She'll still worry,'

'Perhaps she will, but maybe if she understands why you do it, perhaps she'll understand a bit more too?'

'I think it's probably partly because I'm an only child. They would have liked more children, I think, and I'd certainly have loved having brothers and sisters; but it wasn't meant to be. We've never really spoken about it, but I think that's at the root of it.' Maggie paused for a moment. 'So, do you have brothers or sisters?'

'No, I'm an only child too.'

'And are your parents protective of you?'

'I never really knew my parents,' said Cliff, taking another sip of his drink.

'Oh I'm so sorry,' said Maggie quickly. 'I keep putting my foot in it.'

'Don't worry,'

'But here I am complaining about my overprotective mother, and you, well you lost your mum.'

'It was a long time ago. I never knew her at all; she died just after I was born, and then my father died about 18 months later. I was told he died of a broken heart because he'd lost my mother.'

'How sad.'

'Yes and no,' said Cliff. 'Oh course it was sad to lose my mother, but it meant my father gave me a lot of attention when I was a baby. Even though I was very young when he died, I have loads of photos of us playing together in the garden, and he seemed to take me everywhere with him. There are photographs of him playing golf and giving me piggy-back rides. There are holiday pictures of us at the seaside with giant sandcastles and paddling together and picnics.'

'You do seem to have such happy memories.'

'I don't know if they're real memories or it's just what I see in the photos.'

'So who brought you up when he died?' asked Maggie.

'He had a brother, my Uncle Bob. So when my father died, I went to live with him. But he was single, and I was still in nappies and little more than a toddler, so he employed a housekeeper-cum-nanny and she looked after me. I always thought Uncle Bob would marry Miss Woodhouse and we'd be a real family, but it never happened.'

'Now I feel sorry for you,' said Maggie lightly but with a serious note in her voice.

'Oh don't be. Alice, that's Miss Woodhouse, was wonderful to me. She and Uncle Bob did everything for me. They were great fun. I suppose I was lucky in a way, because neither of them were my parents and so they weren't so serious, and Alice was always there for me. I suppose she was paid to be, but I never saw it like that.'

'And then what happened?'

'Well, Uncle's health deteriorated about five years ago, and he's just got slower and slower and eventually he died last year, leaving Blackthorn Manor to me and the house where we lived, Dovetail Cottage, to Alice.'

'Dovetail Cottage! I know that; it's the other side of the village, near the school and that new estate,' said Maggie in surprise.

'That's right. My Uncle bought it because he thought I ought to be able to mix with other children, which I did when I went to school. It had a lovely garden, and we'd spend most of the summer holidays camping outside.'

'Is Alice still there now?'

'Oh yes, but she says it's too big just for her. I think she'd like me to move back in so she can look after me, but she's not as young as she used to be, and I think I ought to be looking after her.'

'Will she stay there?'

'I can't see her ever moving. She was thinking of asking her sister to come and stay with her to keep her company, but I think her sister wasn't too keen. So why do you know Dovetail Cottage?' asked Cliff.

Maggie thought for a moment. 'It's an unusual name, and I remember it's a pretty house with garden all the way around.' Maggie thought for a while. 'Didn't you used to have a flag flying or something?'

'Yes,' laughed Cliff. 'It was originally a Union Jack, but then I had a pirate party and the Union Jack was exchanged for a Jolly Roger flag which was around for years.'

'Do you still see her?'

'I go and visit, but probably not as often as I should. In fact, she worries that I'm not eating enough or that I'll get ill living at Blackthorn.'

'What's wrong with Blackthorn?' asked Maggie. 'Blackthorn Manor sounds such a grand place.'

'It must have been very grand in its day, but it's been empty for years and needs a lot of work done on it.'

Cliff took out his mobile phone and flicked through his photos on it until he found what he was looking for.

'Is this Blackthorn Manor?' asked Maggie in surprise. Cliff nodded. 'It's beautiful. It's like a scene from a costume drama. I can just imagine someone pulling up in front in a horse and carriage.'

'That's a romantic view of it. In reality it's too big for me to live in, even if I had a large family. It's just not cost effective. I considered converting it into flats or making it into a hotel, but my heart's not really in that. Then I bumped into a police colleague I used to work with who introduced me to this Christian charity who help drug addicts who've got into trouble with the police due to their addiction. They used to go to the hospital rehab unit, but that's closing now, and so that was the germ of the idea.'

'Tell me more,' invited Maggie as she finished her coffee.

'I can do better than that,' said Cliff.

'Come on, let me show you the place and you can see it for yourself and the plans. Nothing's fixed, so you may come up with some good ideas.' Maggie hesitated. 'I'd value your input, as you obviously come across some addicts who are homeless because of their addiction and have been thrown out of their own homes.'

'OK,' agreed Maggie. 'I've got my car here, so shall I follow you?'

Maggie was pleased to have the cold evening air on her face as she left the hot and stuffy hotel. She hoped it would help her clear her head, but despite driving with the window open, all Maggie could think about was Cliff.

I don't need a man in my life, Maggie told herself firmly as she drove along behind Cliff in his sports car. *He may be handsome and charming, but I like my freedom, and I certainly don't want to be tied down. I like my independence,* declared Maggie as she thought about her plans to leave Haddon Hall and buy herself a place of her own not too far away, but just far enough to have a life of her own.

She and her father had already looked at Church Cottage, which had recently been refurbished. It was a lovely little place, but right on the doorstep of Haddon Hall and far too close, thought Maggie, to her mother.

After about half an hour, Cliff's car pulled off the main road and onto a narrow single track road which led to a drive up to Blackthorn Manor. The house was stone-built and lit up by a number of spotlights aimed at the front.

*   *   *

At a quick glance, the house looked just as it did in the photo on Cliff's phone, but on taking a second glance, Maggie noticed some broken windows and scaffolding holding up the whole of the right side as you faced the property.

'What do you think?' asked Cliff.

'It's got potential,' said Maggie after a while.

'It's too dark for you to see properly, but the grounds are the best bit. I've got 20 acres.'

'Wow!' said Maggie as she followed Cliff up to the main entrance of the manor. 'Is it safe?' she asked.

'It's structurally sound,' said Cliff as he switched on a large chandelier which lit up a large hallway with an elegant sweeping staircase.

'It's beautiful,' said Maggie.

'But?' asked Cliff. 'I think I detected something?'

'It reminds me of Haddon Hall, which has always been too big for the three of us, though we always have someone staying or some function going on.'

Cliff did a quick tour of the manor house. The rooms had large ceilings and big airy windows, but it was terribly cold and uninviting. It had not been decorated in years, and in Maggie's opinion it was missing a woman's touch.

'So?' said Cliff.

'Well you haven't shown me your plans yet, but I can see that it would be best to convert it into a hotel or hostel. You've got so many bedrooms, and then downstairs a communal dining room and a lounge, and then there's the library, study and kitchen. I'd keep the drawing room as a reception or office, so I wouldn't change the rooms at all, other than modernising and redecorating.'

'Good, that's what I thought.'

'But,' said Maggie, 'I wouldn't want to live here.'

'No, it's not for you,' said Cliff rather briskly. Maggie shot him a look and wondered if he'd been muttering to himself in his car telling himself that he didn't want a woman in his life. 'I hope you're never a drug addict,' he was saying.

They left the house. As they did so, Cliff collected up a box of papers, letters and a torch.

Outside, Maggie followed as Cliff put the box in the boot of his car and then marched off to the side of the main house. The cold night air woke her up. She tried to keep a clear head, and told herself again and again she was just here to give her advice and thoughts on a possible rehabilitation centre, nothing more.

As she went, she couldn't help noticing the little hairs on the back of Cliff's neck, and wondered what it would be like to put her arms around him and pull him towards her to kiss her. She was just beginning another daydream when she heard an owl hoot. The noise brought her back to reality, and she reminded herself she had no need for a man in her life; it would just cause problems and complicate everything. She was happy with the way things were and there was no need to change anything.

They walked for a while, and Maggie wondered where they were going. She was just about to ask when she saw, in the torchlight, another house.

It was a large Victorian-style house

with a central front door and a bay window on each side. The house was set in the centre of a large garden, and the whole plot was hidden behind a wall.

'Who lives here?' asked Maggie. At first she thought it must be Alice, but then remembered she was still at Dovetail Cottage.

'The manor has two houses, this one and a smaller one where I live,' replied Cliff as he opened the front door with a bunch of keys.

The house smelt a bit stale and musty. The floorboards creaked, but there was a pleasant atmosphere about the place.

'Who lived here?' asked Maggie again.

'Years ago it was the cook and the head gardener. The butler and house-keeper lived in the smaller cottage.'

'I thought a butler was more important than a gardener?'

'Depends what your priorities are,' said Cliff as he led Maggie upstairs.

The property had four roomy bedrooms around a central staircase and a large bathroom at the top of the stairs.

'Just like the house, it needs a lot doing to it, but I thought this could be for the staff. The lounge would make a good common room, and the dining room could be a meeting room.'

'No,' said Maggie quickly. 'You can't do that.' Cliff shot her a look. 'Well of course it's your property, and you can do exactly what you like. But it's such a lovely place, it ought to be a home, a family home.'

'But who would want to buy a house so close to a drug rehab place?'

'People who work with your inmates?'

'Well, that's what I meant,' said Cliff.

'But you were talking about a common room and a meeting room. I meant having a family, a real family living there.'

'Nice idea,' said Cliff, who obviously was not convinced.

There was an awkward silence for a little while.

'I'd love to see it properly in

daylight,' said Maggie.

Cliff said little as he locked up and led Maggie back past the manor house.

'It's easier to drive as I've got that box,' said Cliff unlocking his car and holding the passenger's door open for Maggie. 'Your car will be fine here.'

They drove down a path that Maggie hadn't even noticed before. It was on the opposite side of the manor house and led to a small wood. It was very dark. Maggie peered through the windscreen but could see nothing but blackness.

She was all too aware of Cliff's body close to her as she sat beside him in his little sports car, watching his hands as he changed gears and flicked on the main headlights. She could hear the gentle rhythm of his breathing, and caught a faint smell of his aftershave, and again had to fight the desire to reach out and touch him.

Suddenly the wood broke into a little clearing, and there was a smaller version of the lovely Victorian house they had just left.

The door creaked as Cliff turned the key with one hand while balancing the box of papers from the manor house on his knee.

As soon as he switched on the light, Maggie could see that this place was inhabited.

6

Two days later, Maggie had a phone call from Cliff, who was insistent that she should meet him for lunch.

'I'm sorry but I can't make it; I'm busy all day,' said Maggie.

'Busy doing what?' asked Cliff in a way that made Maggie's hackles rise.

'It's not really any of your business,' she said softly. 'But actually, I'm helping sort out a lot of old jumble-sale boxes that have been donated. There's a jumble sale on Saturday in the village hall, and a lot of it needs sorting and probably cleaning or mending.'

'Well you'll have to stop sometime for lunch,' argued Cliff. 'I'll come and pick you up. We can have lunch in that pub across the road from the church.'

'I was just going to have a sandwich with the ladies,' said Maggie.

'Look, Maggie,' said Cliff, 'I really

need a word with you. Can't you just spare half an hour?'

There was something about the way he pleaded that made her give in. She was intrigued to know what it was he wanted and why it was so urgent.

At one o'clock on the dot, Cliff beeped his horn outside the village hall. It made Maggie cross, although she had spent all morning being teased because during the first hour of sorting out the jumble she'd mentioned Cliff's name five times, and her best friend Angela had picked up on this.

'That'll be your young man,' said Angela. Maggie blushed and made a quick exit.

Cliff parked his little sports car in the pub car park. Maggie crossed the road and met him as he was checking he'd locked the doors.

Cliff ordered them both a bowl of homemade soup and a roll. They sat in a cosy corner of the pub.

'So what's this all about?' asked Maggie.

'I need your help,' said Cliff, looking around him and then leaning forward so that when he whispered, no one else could hear what was being said. 'Things are beginning to move forward my end. I've got a team of builders in to repair and redecorate the house.'

'Not the family house?' asked Maggie anxiously.

'No, the manor, of course,' said Cliff a little crossly. 'I was interviewing for a project manager the other day. There were two men, both ex-addicts, but clean, I believe. I've definitely seen one at your tea bar. I think they've both been there.'

'So what do you want from me?'

'I want some more information about them,' replied Cliff simply. 'Inside information.'

'I can't do that,' said Maggie straight away. 'I couldn't break the confidentiality rule. Anything anyone tells me is confidential; I can't pass it on.'

'What if they were dealing? Surely you'd have to tell the police.'

'I couldn't,' said Maggie. 'But some

of our volunteers are special police officers, and I can't say what they'd do. My job is only to serve teas and make people feel welcome. Sometimes it's the only smile they get.'

'That's all very well,' said Cliff dismissively. 'But I've got a real job opportunity for one man, and I have two candidates, and I want to make the right choice. I thought you'd be able to help me.'

'Well I can't,' said Maggie adamantly. If Cliff had not already ordered the soup, she felt she would have walked out then.

The waitress brought over their meals, and for a few minutes they were quiet while they ate.

'At least listen to the descriptions,' said Cliff. Maggie shrugged her shoulders. She really did not want to pry into other people's lives.

'I don't want to be a spy or betray any trust,' she said again.

'I understand that, but don't you see — you could help someone get a really good job. I'm willing to pay well because I want the right person. I want an ex-addict who knows what it's really like and what will work.'

'I'm sorry, I just not prepared to — '

'What if I replaced your tea bar?' said Cliff.

Maggie was tempted for a moment, but Paulo had texted her that morning to say he had heard about a mobile food unit that was going for a reasonable rate. He was planning to have a good look at it with a mechanic friend of his and would let Maggie know later on that day.

'I can't,' she said. 'It just feels so disloyal, and I couldn't live with myself.'

Cliff let out a deep sigh. 'OK. Just listen to me; you don't need to say any-thing, but maybe you'll go away and think about what I've said.' Maggie nodded. 'There are two men. Joe Malone is older, in his forties but looks older. He's got deep wrinkles all over his face.'

'I know Joe,' said Maggie quietly.

'Good, now we're getting somewhere.'

'I only said I know him, I didn't say I'd agreed to give you any information.'

'For goodness sake Maggie, just listen,' said Cliff in a hoarse whisper. 'The other guy is much younger, only 24, but really enthusiastic. His girlfriend's expecting a baby and he's so keen to get a job and provide a home. He's known as Tash because of his really long and dark moustache, like a Mexican.'

'I know Tash and Em, his girlfriend.'

'Excellent,' said Cliff. 'I thought I'd recognised them both from your tea bar, but don't worry, I didn't mention your name or anything about you, so they'll never know there's a connection between us.'

'*Is* there a connection?' asked Maggie, looking up into Cliff's twinkling blue eyes. He flashed her a sharp, hurt look, as though he were penetrating deep inside her to fathom her out. He had no chance to answer because the waitress approached their table.

'Is the soup all right?' she asked with a smile aimed mainly at Cliff.

'It's lovely,' he said automatically, returning her smile. 'Thank you.'

The waitress disappeared. Cliff finished his soup and looked seriously at Maggie.

'I'm sure you can understand, the last thing I want to do is to trust someone with this job and then find they're back on drugs and are no use to me at all.'

'You've interviewed them,' said Maggie. 'Isn't that enough to make up your mind?'

'I'll be honest with you. I want to offer it to Tash, he's so keen, but Joe's got more experience and lots of contacts. I was hoping you'd be able to add just a snippet of information that would help me make the right choice.'

Cliff gave her an appealing look with big eyes and sad face.

'It's no use you giving me those puppy eyes. I've told you I have my principles, and there's absolutely no way I'll change my mind. Do you understand that? There's nothing you can say, so don't even try!'

'You're so beautiful when you're angry and passionate about something,' laughed Cliff.

'It's no joking matter,' said Maggie crossly, although she loved it when Cliff told her she looked beautiful. She looked at her watch, although she didn't see what time it actually said. 'I need to go. We've got so much still to do.' Maggie stood up and collected up her belongings. 'Thank you for lunch, but I'm sorry I can't help you.'

★　★　★

Maggie was quiet all afternoon. The teasing continued but this time she didn't respond.

'They must have had a lovers' tiff at lunchtime,' Angela said to another lady, in front of Maggie.

'He's not my lover,' said Maggie. 'He's just a . . . well he's not even a friend. Just someone I've bumped into a few times lately.'

'But very handsome.'

'Looks aren't everything,' said Maggie, and several of the other ladies nodded in agreement.

'Nice car though,' said one. 'He must have some money. What job does he do?'

'He works with drug addicts,' said Maggie, giving more information than she'd intended. 'Look, we had a laugh this morning, but could we just talk about something else now?' she pleaded, and the conversation changed to more general, light-hearted things.

By six o'clock, they finished the last of the boxes and set up the hall for the jumble sale.

'I feel so dusty,' said Maggie as she washed her hands. 'I can't wait to go home for a shower.'

'I'm really sorry if I upset you earlier,' said Angela. 'I didn't mean to. It's just I was so delighted to think you'd found a lovely young man. I mean, you do so much for other people, it's about time you had some love in your own life.'

'He's not a boyfriend or anything,' repeated Maggie. 'Honestly, I've only met him a couple of times, and although we generally get on OK, we certainly don't agree on everything.'

'When are you seeing him again?'

'We haven't any plans to see each other again. I may never see him.'

'And how does that make you feel?'

Maggie thought for a moment. She remembered how much she'd missed him when he hadn't come to the tea bar last weekend. She realised she'd miss him, but she also knew her pride would stop her contacting him, and so it would be up to him to contact her.

'I'm so busy at the moment, I don't really have time for a man in my life.'

'If you say so,' said Angela. 'Anyway, I just wanted to apologise if I upset you. I really didn't mean to.'

'No problem,' said Maggie, giving her best friend a smile. 'We really ought to go out together sometime.'

'That would be great, although Dad's not doing too well at the moment. His memory is worse than ever. He seems to have forgotten he's retired. He got up for work the other morning and we had quite an argument when I told him he'd sold his car.'

'Well, perhaps I could bring an old film over, one that he'd like to watch too, and we could have a night in?' suggested Maggie.

'That would be great,' agreed Angela. 'I'll look forward to it.'

They'd walked to the point where they would each go their separate ways. Maggie hesitated. 'I was thinking about Jessie the other day,' she said quietly. 'Have you ever heard from her?'

'Not a word,' Angela told her. 'As if it isn't hard enough having lost Mum and caring for Dad, I could really do with Jessie's support.'

Maggie could see Angela's eyes filling up with tears. 'I'm sorry. I didn't mean to stir up everything.'

'I'd just like to know she was safe. I don't know how I'd react if I saw her. I feel so angry and yet I miss her so much.'

Maggie remembered what had happened when Jessie had first left. Angela had done everything she could to try and track her down, but she'd vanished. She'd had even gone to the police to report her missing, but because the two of them had argued and they were both still grieving the loss of their mother, they weren't taken very seriously. Apparently people went missing every day, and if someone didn't want to be found, then it wasn't so hard to disappear.

Maggie gave her friend a hug and made her way home, wondering whether it could have been Jess she saw at the tea bar.

7

'I think you've got something to tell me,' Nancy announced as they sat down to Sunday lunch.

Maggie glanced at her father, who shrugged. She knew she needed to come clean and tell her mother the truth about her work with the homeless. In an ideal world, she would have liked to have been the one to start the conversation, because by then she would have had it planned out in her head. Her mother had caught her unawares.

'So,' continued Nancy, 'when were you going to tell me?'

'I have tried,' Maggie said.

'I would have found out sooner or later. I'd have heard something or seen muddy paws. You can't hide a dog forever. I just wish we'd had a proper conversation about getting a pet before you'd gone and done it behind my back.'

Maggie and her father exchanged looks once more. Robert shrugged again, but this time neither of them had any idea what Nancy was talking about.

'Pardon?' Maggie asked. 'Do you think I've got a pet?' She laughed at the thought of keeping a hamster in her room.

'I know you've got a dog,' Nancy said, 'so there's no use denying it.'

'A dog?' echoed Maggie. 'I really don't know what you're talking about. Honestly, I haven't got a dog, and believe me, I would have chatted to you about it first.'

'I'm sorry, Margaret,' Nancy said in a shrill voice. 'I hate to say this, but I don't believe you.'

'What makes you think Maggie's got a dog?' Robert asked calmly, obviously trying to keep the peace between his wife and daughter.

'She's been buying dog food. I've seen it in her room, although why you need so many can openers, I really don't know.'

'Oh Mum!' Maggie laughed, relieved to be accused of something she was totally innocent of. 'The dog food was on special offer and I bought to donate to several homeless people who have dogs.'

'Surely you're only homeless if you have no money,' Nancy said. 'I think it's irresponsible to have a dog when you haven't got the means to feed it or look after it properly.'

'People don't choose to become homeless!' Maggie snapped, but she could see her father out of the corner of her eye and knew she had to try to smooth things over. 'I imagine that if you have to sleep on a park bench or in a doorway, you'd feel safer if you had a dog to protect you. Don't you think?'

'I dare say you're right, but — '

'And if you snuggled up to your dog, it would help keep you warm. And they're good company. But don't worry, Mum; I've no plans to get a dog. At least not until I have a place of my own.'

'So you aren't hiding a dog?'

'Definitely not,' Maggie confirmed as she concentrated on eating her roast beef. 'This is delicious. Do you want another roastie, Dad?'

Between them, Maggie and her father moved the conversation away from dogs and the homeless on to general, safe topics; but for the rest of the day, there was a bit of an atmosphere about the home.

Maggie was pleased to slip out and take an old film over to Angela's to watch with her and her father. She told her mother she was staying with Angela for supper and wouldn't be back until later.

On Sunday evening, Maggie drove in to the city centre in her little Citroën fully stocked with as many flasks of hot water as she could borrow. She had tea bags, coffee, milk, sugar, and a selection of biscuits.

She also had a box of tinned dog

food and half a dozen can openers. She was glad her mother hadn't seen her loading up the car and resumed their conversation. As much as Maggie was now keen to get everything out in the open, she knew now would not be a good time. But would she be forever finding a reason to put it off?

It had been raining all day, but now the rain had stopped and it was just cloudy and overcast. However, Maggie's mood was unusually low, and she felt miserable for no good reason. This made her cross with herself because she was usually such a jolly, positive person and proud to feel she could cheer people up. And yet today she'd woken up with a feeling of a great weight upon her shoulders, and no matter how she tried, she did not seem to be able to shift it.

Lunch with her parents had only made matters worse, and spending the afternoon with Angela and her aging father had made her sad. But she hoped she'd have a chance to see Jess; and if she did, she'd do her best to get her to contact her sister.

'Hello!' she said cheerfully to Dee, who had just parked in the layby and was opening up her car boot.

'No flat tyres this time,' said Dee. 'But have you heard about Paulo?'

'No,' said Maggie with an even deeper feeling of dread.

'His van's been stolen from right outside his home. Can you believe it?'

'Well at least he wasn't hurt,' said Maggie quickly. She then remembered he was meant to have called her after he'd been to see if the mobile food unit was any good. 'He was supposed to call me the other day.'

'He said he'd try and make it tonight, but obviously won't be able to bring all his stuff. It was all taken. He was hoping he'd get a lift from a friend.'

'Oh well, I've got lots of hot water and everything else we need,' said Maggie. 'But it'll be useful to have an extra pair of hands.'

Once again, Maggie helped Dee set

up. She'd brought an old decorating table and used that to serve her crock pots of stew, while Maggie used a large tray over the top of a concrete rubbish bin. It wasn't ideal, but the fact that she was there and able to offer some hot refreshment to those living rough was the important thing. For some, it was more important to have a bit of company and see a friendly face.

Most people wanted Dee's stew, and lined up for that. Maggie noticed one young girl with a big bruise on the side of her face. Last time she'd seen the girl, there was no bruise, but she'd had her arm in a sling.

'Hello, Tina,' said Maggie. 'Glad to see your arm's better. Can I pour you a tea?'

'Thanks.'

Maggie noticed as she handed over the hot tea that not only did she have a bruised cheek, but one of her front teeth was missing. She was tempted to ask what had happened, but knew it wasn't anything to do with her, and she had no right to pry into Tina's business. She knew Tina or one of the others would tell her if they wanted her to know.

There was a different atmosphere tonight. Maggie thought at first that it was just her low mood and what Dee had told her about Paulo's van. And, she had to admit, the fact that once again there was no sign of Cliff.

'Have you heard?' said Teabag. 'John's died.'

John was a nineteen-year-old lad who'd been living rough for about a year. His parents had thrown him out of their home when he'd been caught shoplifting in order to get money to buy drugs. He'd been in and out of hospital as much as he'd been in and out of police cells. His parents had been supportive initially, but he'd gone from recreational drugs to the hard stuff. He'd stolen from his parents and told them a string of lies. They'd taken as much as they could. It had probably broken their hearts to close the door to their son, but maybe they thought they were being cruel to be kind.

Last time Maggie had seen John, they'd had a very strange conversation, because one minute he was alert and answered her questions about some work he'd been doing with Paulo, and then almost without warning he seemed to slip into semi-consciousness and didn't know where he was or what time of day it was. His skin was pale and his eyes had great black shadows under them. His hands shook, and he was always cold, even when the sun shone and people complained of the heat. Maggie then remembered he'd been talking with Joe Malone and they'd had a big argument.

Maggie looked up from the flask she'd been pouring and noticed Joe talking earnestly to a man in a long grey coat. She looked about and her eyes fell on Tash. He'd already fetched two cups of tea and had taken them over to Emma, his girlfriend. He'd found her a seat and he was now standing beside her with an arm resting gently on her shoulder.

Paulo arrived with a big box of sandwiches donated by Pret a Manger. Brian, another volunteer, offered to help Maggie pour teas. They soon got through the crowd. There weren't so many people today, and the atmosphere was very subdued as if in respect for young John.

'Will you be all right for a moment?' Maggie asked Brian. 'I just want to chat to a few people.'

'I'll be fine,' he replied.

'Those flasks are empty, but those two are full,' said Maggie as she wandered over to Tash and Em. 'How are you keeping?' she asked Emma, looking down at her growing womb.

'Ok,' said Em. 'I can feel it moving around now.' They chatted for a while about the baby, and Maggie promised to bring some baby clothes.

'You keep hold of them until it's born,' said Em. 'We've got nowhere to store anything, but Tash is hoping to get a job with a room.'

'I'm a bit worried about Tina,' said Maggie, not wanting to let on she knew anything about a job.

'He's hit her again,' said Em. 'I don't know why she stays with him! I suppose it's the drugs.'

Maggie glanced over again at Tina and noticed she was hovering around Joe Malone.

'That's a nasty bruise she's got,' said Maggie. 'And she's got a tooth missing.'

'Joe lost it the other night when the pub was raided.' Maggie was just about to confirm that it was Joe Malone when a pair of police officers appeared. Maggie's attention was diverted for a matter of seconds, but when she looked back in Joe's direction, he was nowhere to be seen.

Maggie chatted to the policemen about the burnt-down tea bar. Everyone seemed to accept it was burnt down by the publican of the Red Lion, but there was no proof. She couldn't put her finger on it, but there was something different about the manner of the police this time. Normally they were left alone. Occasionally a uniformed officer would come and just pass the time of day with her 'clients' as they ate their free stew or drank their tea, but today they seemed less friendly, more business-like.

'There's a new chief,' said one of the specials. 'He's young and keen to make his mark. He's already made lots of changes. I think he means well, but he doesn't know the area and all he's doing is stirring up trouble. They're really clamping down on drug pushers.'

'I heard about John,' said Maggie. She listened to the special police officer chatting with the group huddled round the coffee. They were all expecting trouble, and even suggested that perhaps it would be better not to serve tea for a few weeks.

Maggie was about to say something, but Tina caught her eye. She was hobbling away. Maggie was shocked. The woman was only in her late twenties but looked more like an old woman. Maggie suspected she was covering up more injuries.

'Do you need me to take you to casualty?' asked Maggie as she easily caught up with Tina.

'I'm fine,' said Tina, looking scared as she glanced around, possibly looking for Joe, who'd completely disappeared as soon as the police walked by.

'You're not fine,' said Maggie. 'It's none of my business what — '

'No,' said Tina fiercely, 'it's none of your business.' With that she walked away, and Maggie knew she had tried but could do no more tonight.

That evening as she drove away from the city with her empty flasks, Maggie thought about what she knew of Joe Malone. He was a slimy character. His fingers dripped with heavy gold knuckle-duster rings. He wore a large gold chain round his neck and an equally hefty gold bracelet. He always looked shifty, but seemed to help others, often the young lads like John and Tash. Now she was questioning whether he was actually helping them, or helping himself. How naive she'd been.

It dawned on Maggie that Joe was obviously not homeless himself, and now she remembered that Tina had mentioned she'd found a flat and that Joe had been involved. Maggie hadn't realised Tina meant she'd moved in with Joe, but now she knew that was what had happened, and it looked like he was abusing her.

She realised too, now that she thought about it, that many of the regulars appeared to avoid Joe. Most people greeted each other with a hug or a shake of the hand. Everyone knew everyone else's name; but Joe, now she pictured the scene, always stood on the edge and just drew off one young man or another. It was always the young and vulnerable, just like poor John. Just like Tina.

Maggie pulled up at All Saints Church and slipped in quietly. She said a little prayer for John and his family.

She added the names of Tina, Tash and Em on the end of her prayer and realised that she could actually do something positive to help Tash and Em and the unborn baby.

She dialled Cliff's number, but it was engaged. She left a vague message on his voicemail.

Now she had decided that she would help Tash, she felt a great deal better about herself, and realised that tonight was the night she would talk to her mother and get that all out in the open. She knew how awful she'd felt at lunchtime when she thought her mother had found her out. This had to stop, and the sooner the better.

She tried Cliff's number again but it was still on voicemail. Maggie rinsed out the flasks in the vestry and then made her way home to Haddon Hall.

As she was looking to see if there was any supper left for her, she noticed the local paper on the breakfast bar. She made herself a cup of coffee and flicked through. On the inside page was a big picture of none other than Cliff Hunter shaking hands with a local developer. Maggie recognised him from the conference and knew he'd made Cliff an offer for his land. The article stated that Cliff had agreed to sell, and plans for 400 houses were being drawn up for the Blackthorn estate.

Her hand shook as she redialled Cliff's number. How could he? It was such a betrayal!

8

Maggie hadn't calmed down at all by the time she eventually spoke to Cliff on his mobile.

'How dare you sell up to that man!' she almost screamed at him.

'You've seen the paper, then?' asked Cliff. His voice sounded cool and calm, as though he lacked any feeling at all. That just added fuel to Maggie's fire.

'You sound as though you don't even care! I thought you were a compassionate man, someone with principles who could make a difference for lots of people — and yet you're just the same as any other man!'

'I do care!' said Cliff with a little more passion. 'Believe me.'

'How *can* I believe you? You promised me you wouldn't sell up, and now less than a week's gone by and you've done the deal. I don't know how you could. I respected you. I admired the fact that you had money but were unselfish enough to use it to help others. How wrong can I be? To think I was falling for you, and now . . . '

'Falling for me? Were you?' asked an amused Cliff.

'Now I hate you!' said Maggie with feeling.

'Will you listen to my side of the story?' asked Cliff patiently. Maggie was about to cut him off and delete his number, but there was something about his voice and the fact that she wanted to believe what he had to say. However, he was going to have to come up with a very convincing story.

'I'd prefer to talk face to face.'

'Forget it,' said Maggie.

'OK, if you insist,' Cliff agreed reluctantly. 'Remember when we were at that conference, and just as we were leaving, the guy shook my hand and someone took a photo?'

'Yes.'

'Well they've used that photo and

concocted the story in the hope that they'll bamboozle me into a sale. But I've spoken to them, and with the newspaper, as well as my solicitor, and a very different story is going out in tomorrow's edition on the front page.'

'Oh,' said Maggie quietly.

'Satisfied? Or will you need to wait until you've seen tomorrows paper for yourself?'

'I just thought . . . ' began Maggie. 'I'm sorry, I should have known better, but I suppose I don't really know you that well at all.'

'And whose fault is that? I keep asking you out and you keep coming up with excuses not to see me!' Cliff was not sounding so cool and calm now, Maggie noticed.

'I tried to phone you several times this evening.'

'Just so you could have a go at me?'

'Actually, I've been thinking about what you were asking me the other day, and I had some information to pass on to you.'

'Oh well, it doesn't matter anymore,' said Cliff. Maggie didn't know if he was just being childish and petty or if it really no longer mattered.

'Suit yourself.'

'Don't get like that, Maggie,' said Cliff. 'It's just that I decided to offer Tash the job, but when I rang him he was in a real state. Apparently they'd been to the tea bar and then gone on to the Salvation Army, but there was a big fight. Tash had tried to defend some poor girl who was being beaten up by her boyfriend. Tash tried to stop him, according to him anyway. The guy lashed out, aiming to hit Tash, but he'd been drinking and completely missed, punching Emma in the face and knocking her flying. She fell unconscious with a bleeding nose. They've taken her to hospital because of the baby.'

'Is she OK?' asked Maggie, her voice back to her old self, full of concern.

'I'm not sure, but we could go to the hospital and find out. Shall I come and get you?'

Maggie was about to accept when she caught a glimpse of her mother coming towards her.

'Maybe later. There's something I have to do first. Bye.'

Before Maggie got a chance to speak to her mum, the house phone had rung, and Nancy was busy sorting out dates for a series of meetings.

Maggie sat at the breakfast bar with her coffee. She felt drained. She relived the conversation she'd just had with Cliff and wondered why on earth she'd flown off the handle at him without knowing all the facts. Her emotions were running riot at the moment. Cliff had got under her skin in a way that no one had ever managed to do before.

She looked at the photo again in the paper and could clearly recognise the venue from the other day. She could even make out her own sleeve on the edge of the photo, so she guessed what Cliff had said was true.

She was cross with herself, again, for jumping to the wrong conclusions and then telling Cliff that she had nearly fallen for him, and she blushed with embarrassment.

'Are you all right, Margaret?' asked Nancy when she'd finished on the phone. 'You look tired. You're not sickening for something, are you?'

'I'm fine. I've just had a bad day,' said Maggie. Suddenly tears welled up, and before she knew it, her mother was giving her a hug and the tears began to fall.

'I've got something I've been meaning to tell you for ages,' said Maggie after a while when she'd wiped away her tears.

'So you've got a boyfriend! I knew it. I've told everyone that I thought you had a boyfriend. I knew I was right.'

'I haven't got a boyfriend! Don't jump to conclusions!' Then she said, 'I'm sorry, I didn't mean to snap.'

'That's OK, dear. I know it's not like you. So if you haven't got a boyfriend, what is it?'

'Who have you told?' asked Maggie,

sidetracked by her mother.

'Oh, lots of people. You think I don't notice, but I'm not blind. I see you sneaking off every Sunday afternoon with your bag and then again on a Tuesday. I know you're up to something. I thought you were walking your dog, but obviously I got that wrong.'

'Did you tell Cliff Hunter I had a boyfriend?' asked Maggie. His name was always on her lips, and seemed to trip off her tongue before she even knew she'd said it.

'The young man who came to the charity dinner the other evening?'

'Yes.'

'Yes, I think I did.' She paused and thought for a moment. 'I shouldn't have done, really, because he looked like quite a good catch himself, and I shouldn't have put him off, although maybe that would make you look more attractive.'

'Mother!'

'Margaret, there's no need to shout!'

'Well, what will he think of me if he

thinks I've got a boyfriend?'

'So, is he your boyfriend? I didn't think you knew him, although you did spend a lot of time with him that evening and you saw him again at that business conference you went to, and for drinks afterwards. He seemed very nice. Your father spoke well of him, too.'

'Mum,' said Maggie decisively, 'please sit down.'

Nancy did as she was asked. She sat opposite Maggie and looked at her daughter.

'On a Sunday evening, I go into the city and serve hot drinks to people who live on the streets. On Tuesdays, we use a church hall and serve a hot meal. I don't do it on my own — '

'But that could be so dangerous. Only the other day I read about a fight between some drug addicts. What if they had needles and injected you with something? You could get AIDS and die.'

'It's not like that,' said Maggie, trying to reassure her mother. 'Most of the time there's no trouble at all, and if there is, the police are always very quickly on the scene.'

'And does your father already know about this?'

'He's been begging me to tell you, but I knew you'd react like this. I knew you'd worry, but really there's nothing to worry about. Maybe one evening you could come with me and see for yourself.'

'I certainly don't want to go into the city centre at night, and certainly not with all those criminals around. I forbid you to go again.'

'Mum, they're homeless, not criminal.'

'It's the same thing, I'm sure.'

'Why on earth should it be the same? Some youngsters get involved in drugs at school if they get in with the wrong crowd, and when they're addicted, they need money to pay for drugs.'

'So they steal,' added Nancy.

'They need help,' said Maggie with passion. 'They're not all criminals.

Some girls are chucked out of their homes because they're pregnant or their father abuses them or — '

'Enough!' said Nancy.

Maggie's father arrived at that moment. 'Sorry I'm late. I've been up at the hospital. There's been a big fight up there. Two gangs, I think. Some poor young girl who's expecting a baby was hurt, but she's stable now and looked after by a slip of a thing with a huge black eye and broken tooth.'

Nancy looked at Maggie. 'I'll get Gordon to come and talk to you,' said Nancy, as if that would solve everything.

'I've told her,' Maggie said to her father.

'Good.'

'It's not good, Robert! You've no idea how much danger she's been putting herself in. I'll get Gordon straight away.' Nancy stormed out of the room to find his number. Gordon was an ex-chief of police and an old friend of the family. He had been brought in before to lecture Maggie on the evils of mixing with criminals when Maggie had witnessed a shoplifter some years ago.

'Are you all right?' Robert asked his daughter. 'You look as if you've been crying.'

'I'm fine!' snapped Maggie as she stormed out after her mother and then made her way up to her room.

She threw herself on her bed and cried a few more tears. She had upset the three people she cared most about in the matter of an hour. Her parents arguing downstairs and she knew it was all her fault.

She had been cross with Cliff, and that was also her fault. On top of it, she felt bad about the incident at the hospital. She had pointed out to Tash and Em that she was worried about Tina; maybe that was why Tash had accused Joe of beating her up and the fight had started. Again, all her fault, and she'd only wanted to do good.

Her phone rang. She checked the number and recognised it was Cliff.

Grabbing a handkerchief, she sniffed into it and then answered the call.

'Are you all right?' asked Cliff, sounding really concerned.

'Yes, I'm absolutely fine,' lied Maggie. 'What do you want?'

'I just wanted to check you were OK. I rang the hospital, and they're keeping Emma in overnight. Tash and Tina are with her. At least they'll all be safe on the ward. And I wanted to say sorry.'

'Sorry? Why would you want to say sorry?' asked Maggie, completely mystified.

'Well, it was all a bit of a misunderstanding, and I hate it when we argue.'

Maggie crumbled but tried not to let Cliff hear her sniff as the tears rolled down her cheeks. She had never felt so miserable in her life.

'You'll be pleased to hear I've spoken to my mother and she knows all about the tea bar now.'

'How did that go?'

'It was dreadful. I've upset her, and then I snapped at my poor old dad too.

I'm really not doing anything right tonight.'

'Look,' said Cliff, 'I'm going away for a while. Alice has got a set of keys if you want to get away for a bit and use my place. I know it's a bit of a mess, but use it if you want to have a bit of time to yourself.'

'Thank you. I might just do that. When will you be back?'

'I'm not sure. Something's come up and I need to sort it out, so everything else is now on hold.'

'Oh,' said Maggie, realising she knew very little about Cliff's life really.

'I'll give Alice a ring at Dovetail Cottage and tell her you might call round for the keys.'

'Thanks,' said Maggie again.

She lay on her bed for a while longer and cried a few more tears, then washed her face and began to pack a small bag. Twenty minutes later, she walked down the stairs carrying her overnight bag and wearing a coat.

'And where do you think you're

going?' asked Nancy.

'I'm really sorry I've upset you both, and I certainly didn't mean to. I'm going away for a few days while we all calm down, and then we can talk properly to one another.'

'Where will you go?'

'Don't worry. I'll be staying with a friend. I'll be fine.'

Maggie walked out of the door pretending she was calm, but she didn't dare look back. Once again she had lied to her mother, saying she'd be staying with a friend when she knew she was going to be alone.

Alice was younger than Maggie had expected. Cliff had called her to say it was all right to let Maggie have his keys.

'I've heard so much about you from Cliff,' said Maggie. 'You gave him a really happy childhood, and he's so grateful.'

'And I've heard so much about you from Cliff,' said Alice with a little smile. She handed over the keys. 'I'm sure we'll meet again. Take care.'

Maggie was pleased she didn't have to stay too long with Alice, because all she wanted to do was to curl up and sleep.

She found Cliff's home quite easily, but the small path from the manor house to his little cottage was darker than she remembered, and it felt spooky and deadly quiet.

The house was in a state. Cliff was obviously not the tidiest person in the world, but Maggie was relieved to feel safe in his sanctuary and happily closed and locked the door. She made herself a cup of tea and intended on making herself a bed on the sofa. She didn't dare sleep in Cliff's bed.

Once she'd drunk the tea and found a blanket for the sofa, she felt more wide awake. It wasn't very warm in the house, and she slipped on one of Cliff's jumpers. It was a lovely feeling, like having his arms wrapped around her to keep her safe.

Maggie wandered around his home. It was sparse and masculine. On a table she found some files and the plans for Blackthorn Manor. She opened out the plans and had a better look.

There were also designs for the large Victorian house that she had fallen in love with. She sat at his table and began to think what she would do if she had that place.

A bang on the door jolted her awake. Someone was trying to break in! They must know Cliff was away. Maggie slid onto the floor and crawled under the table, feeling safer but rather like a coward.

The noise continued at the doorway, and then it flew open and in stumbled a man. Maggie could make out his big feet and legs, but that was all she could see from her position under the table.

'Maggie?' called the unmistakeable voice of Cliff.

She crawled out from under the table. Cliff was hidden behind a huge bouquet of red roses and a large bottle of champagne.

'Cliff?'

He put down the flowers and bottle and opened his arms to welcome her. 'You sounded so upset, I couldn't leave you alone.' He hugged her and kissed the top of her hair.

It felt so good to Maggie to be held in his arms. She felt protected, and as if Cliff could somehow magically make everything all right.

'I see you've got the plans out,' he said, 'and you're wearing my jumper. Are you cold?'

'I was,' confessed Maggie. 'But I'm fine now.'

Cliff stepped back, but Maggie held on to him and buried her head in his chest.

'What's wrong?' he asked, sounding concerned.

'I was just frightened,' admitted Maggie, trying to make light of things. 'It's been such an awful day. I tried to help Tina and she turned me away. Then I snapped at you, and although it's good I've spoken to my mum, I know I've upset both her and Dad, and

I just feel so . . . ' Maggie dropped her shoulders and did her best to hold back the tears.

'Hey,' said Cliff gently. 'Anyone who knows you even a little bit will know you didn't mean to hurt anyone.'

He put his index finger under her chin and raised her face up to look at him. 'Don't look so sad,' he said. 'I could hear you on the phone and I just wanted to give you a hug.' He bent his head down. His lips found hers. They were soft, but there was a sense of urgency and passion there. Maggie was aware of how quickly she responded. How right it felt to be in his arms at last.

'What do you think?' Cliff asked, glancing down at the plans.

'The kiss or the plans?' asked Maggie with a smile.

'You don't know how long I've wanted to kiss you,' admitted Cliff. He kept his arm around her shoulder as they leaned over the table.

'I hope you don't mind me looking,'

said Maggie, feeling very humble. 'I must admit I only had a peep at the plans for the Victorian house. I love that place.'

'And what do you think?'

'Well, I'd make that extension to the lounge a bit longer and give it a flat roof.' Maggie paused and grabbed a bit of scrap paper. 'I'd then make it into a balcony from the master bedroom. You could change the window in the bedroom into patio doors and put railings round the roof. There would be excellent views of the grounds of Blackthorn Manor.'

'Anything else?' laughed Cliff as he eased the cork out of the champagne.

'I'd put a vegetable garden here, a swing for the children there, and that tree would make an excellent tree house. I've always wanted a tree house.'

'For us, or for our children?' asked Cliff with a laugh.

'For the children!' said Maggie, and then she realised what they'd said. She felt she'd fallen into his trap, but it felt good to laugh together and to flirt and be playful. Had she gone too far?

There was an awkward silence. Maggie noticed the bottle of champagne Cliff was holding. It was the same make that her mother had bought for the fundraising evening, and Maggie knew there were lots of bottles left over.

'Is it just a coincidence, or is that bottle from my parents?' she asked.

'I admit I've been to see your parents. They were really worried about you, but I needed to speak to your father about — '

'How dare you? I trusted you. I thought you were being so kind offering me shelter, but it was just to get me out of the way so you could go behind my back!'

'I didn't mean — '

'I just needed a bit of time away to think. That's typical of Mum — rather than understanding that I needed a bit of time, she sent you round with champagne. We're living on two different planets.'

Maggie didn't even look round for

her bag, but grabbed her car keys and stormed out of the house.

Her car wouldn't start properly the first time, which just made her even more cross. Without thinking, she drove away from Cliff's house, and only when she reached the end of the drive did she wonder where she could go. Tonight she was homeless. She'd left her bag at Cliff's. She had no money on her to pay for a hotel. But her pride would prevent her from going home or returning to Cliffs. That was ironic, she thought, but Maggie knew exactly where she should go.

She headed straight for the nearest church. She thought she'd settle down on a wooden pew for the night.

It was chilly inside, but better than being out in the cold. She was grateful for Cliff's warm jumper, even though she could still smell his aftershave on it.

The church was dark inside, but the moon lit up strange patterns as it filtered through the stained-glass windows. They cast eerie shadows on the flagstone floor.

The wooden pew was uncomfortable, and Maggie was cold; but despite all that, it was the realisation that she was in love with Cliff that kept her awake.

She'd only been there about half an hour when the vicar came to lock up. 'You can't stay here, I'm afraid,' he said, not unkindly. 'I have to lock up. You never know who'd creep in and steal from the collection box.'

Maggie was about to argue, but had realised that the pew was uncomfortable and she was already cold. She wondered if he'd put her up at his vicarage, but she'd probably have to confess she was Rev. Brown's daughter, and that would only end up causing him embarrassment. She couldn't do that to her father.

'Don't worry,' she said. 'I was just going. Good night.'

9

Despite being late, Maggie knew she could call on Angela.

'I'm so sorry,' she said, 'but can I stay the night?'

'Of course,' said Angela, stepping back and holding her dog's collar so he wouldn't jump up at their unexpected guest.

Angela made them both a cup of tea while Maggie explained her eventful day.

Maggie put her face in her hands. 'Now I've told it all to you, I don't know why I stormed out. I've never felt so emotional. One minute I'm as high as a kite and feel the world is so wonderful, and then the next minute I'm down in the dumps and feel everyone is against me. I just don't know what's going on.'

Maggie fiddled about in her pocket for a tissue. She pulled out a screwed-up leaflet she'd picked up from the church.

'I found this,' she said, showing it to Angela. A charity was advertising for volunteers to come and work in a Romanian orphanage. 'I thought it might be a good idea if I did something like this.'

'Are you sure?' asked Angela in surprise. 'You were talking about teacher training and working with adults. I thought that sounded a good idea, being able to pass on your floristry skills.'

'I just feel I need to get away and do something useful.'

'I'm sure it's a good cause, but don't you remember how homesick you were when you went on Guide camp?'

'That was years ago,' said Maggie, but she did remember how dreadful she felt being away from the people and the places she loved.

Angela patted her shoulder. 'Never mind now. I'll go and make up a bed in the spare room. Hopefully you'll feel much better after a good night's sleep.'

Maggie slept in the following morning, but felt all the better for it.

'Here,' said Angela, passing her a large mug of tea. 'Fancy some toast?'

'Toast would be lovely, thank you.' Maggie watched as Angela popped some bread into the toaster and fetched butter and marmalade. 'I needed a good sleep,' admitted Maggie. 'It's done me the world of good.'

'Great. I think my Dad had a good night too, he came down this morning all bright and cheerful and has been pottering round the garden ever since. I think it helped having you round the other day. Sometimes it's not good just being the two of us here. We get on each other's nerves at times.'

Maggie was surprised to hear this, but realised that was what was happening in her own home. She took her tea and chatted with Angela's father for a little while as she ate her toast.

'Thank you so much,' said Maggie again. 'Would you mind if I disappeared now? I've got things I need to do.'

'Of course,' said Angela. 'You're always welcome here, you know that.'

Maggie's plan was to post off her application form to the Romanian charity and then to offer to take Angela's dog for a long walk. However, just as she was entering the post office for a stamp, she bumped into Cliff, who was there buying copies of the local paper. He made no comment that she was still wearing the clothes she'd worn the previous night, including his jumper.

'Look!' he said, pointing to his picture on the front page with a big heading of 'Sorry'.

'I'm sorry too,' said Maggie quietly.

'Don't worry,' he said, and opened his arms. This time Maggie didn't fall into them.

'I don't know what you must think of me. I understand my mother told you I had a boyfriend, and yet I let you kiss me.'

'Talking of kisses . . . ' said Cliff, reaching out for her again.

'I don't have a boyfriend,' continued Maggie. 'In fact there's absolutely no one in my life at the moment, and I don't ever expect there will be.'

'Oh,' said Cliff. 'That sounds lonely.'

Maggie shrugged.

'So, have you done anything about applying for that teacher training you were talking about?'

'No,' said Maggie. 'I'm hoping to go away for a while, so I won't be doing that training this year.'

'Away?' said Cliff in surprise. 'But so many people need you here.'

For a third time he opened up his arms to her, and this time she let him give her a farewell hug. 'Goodbye,' she said.

'Don't say that,' said Cliff. 'I thought we could go for a walk and try to patch things up. You never gave me a chance to explain last night.'

'There's nothing to explain. I'd be grateful if you'd drop my things round to Haddon Hall sometime,' Maggie said. 'Bye.'

She moved away and walked up to the post office counter. She bought a stamp and posted off her application form. If she wasn't successful with this job, she would try another and another. She knew she just had to get away. Besides, she thought, it was time she proved to Angela and her own parents that she'd grown up and was no longer a homesick little girl.

Cliff bought his papers and disappeared. He was obviously on a mission to clear his name.

Maggie returned to Angela's, and together they went on a long walk. She and Angela had known each other since they'd been at school together, and soon Maggie realised that running away was not the answer.

'I've already posted the letter,' Maggie admitted. 'And worse than that, I've said goodbye to Cliff. I thought falling in love would be wonderful, but it's all so confusing and painful. I just don't know which way to turn. I feel I don't even know myself anymore.' Maggie managed to laugh at herself. 'Life used to be so simple,' she said.

'Would you go back?' asked Angela.

'Back to a time before you'd met him?' Maggie thought for a moment, but only for a moment.

'I can't even think back to before Cliff was in my life. I hardly know him really but he's had such a big impact on me.'

'Perhaps you and he ought to . . . ' began Angela, but at that moment Maggie's mobile rang. She had an urgent message from Paulo, as he was supposed to do the Tea Bar tonight.

'I know it's not your usual night, but I can't make it. I thought I had a lift but I've been let down. Neither Pete nor Jane can do it; they've both got a tummy bug. Brian's not answering his phone, and Dee's away with her son.'

'Don't worry,' said Maggie. 'I can do it. I'll go and fill the flasks straight away.'

Maggie looked at her watch. Time was getting on. They usually served tea from 5pm, and it was nearly 4.30pm already.

'Have you got any thermos flasks I

can borrow?' asked Maggie. She explained what she needed them for.

They filled a couple of thermos flasks and the containers Maggie kept in the boot of her car. 'It's not ideal; the water should be hot enough for a coffee, but it's not so good for tea.'

Maggie thought it was odd when she arrived in the city centre and it was really quiet. For a moment she wondered if it was a different time on different nights, but she knew it was always the same time. So where was everyone? She knew something was wrong but was not sure what. She was busy because she was on her own. She was so used to having Dee and Paulo around.

Maggie set up and thought the sooner they replaced the shed or got a mobile van with facilities to heat up the water, the better.

Maggie noticed a policeman walk by, and then another. A patrol car drove past and parked in the layby. It was unusual to have such a high police presence. She wondered what had been going on in town. An ambulance siren wailed in the distance. Perhaps there had been an accident? There was definitely an atmosphere in the air, and it was the first time she'd ever felt vulnerable.

She remembered when she had spoken to her mother the previous evening and foolishly invited her to join her. It was ironic that now, for the very first time in the two years she'd been helping, she felt a little scared.

'This water's not hot,' someone complained.

'Sorry,' said Maggie. 'It's the best I could do tonight.'

The man threw away his drink. It splashed up someone else's trouser leg, and they yelped in surprise.

Maggie packed up her things and almost threw them in the back of the car. 'I'll go and see if I can get some boiling water,' she said, and ran off to ask for help.

No one, it seemed had hot water available. Maggie returned about ten minutes later, empty-handed.

People were milling about, waiting for hot drinks and sandwiches. But Maggie had nothing to offer. She wanted to get in her car and drive off, but then she saw the man pull out a knife.

10

The man with the knife was swaying as he shouted, and his speech was slurred. But when another man stepped forward to try and disarm him, the knife man seemed to become awake and alert and made to stab the person nearest him. A woman screamed, but Maggie couldn't tell if anyone had been hurt, although she felt it was only a matter of time.

A crowd of people emerged from the nearby Red Lion. Maggie had never found the locals at the Red Lion to be either friendly or helpful. They never filled up her flasks with hot water, and they were openly prejudiced against those less fortunate than themselves. This evening they too had been drinking. They could see the crowd and hear the screams. It was plain to see that the knife man and the chap who'd tried to disarm him were almost ready to fight. The atmosphere was fizzing.

'Fight!' shouted one person.

'Fight!' chanted another and then another, as the Red Lion drinkers whipped the crowd into a frenzy.

'Stop!' called Maggie. 'Someone will get hurt!' But no one seemed to hear her. 'Stop!' she shouted again, and she tried to push her way to the front of the crowd but without success.

Maggie hoped that at any minute now the police would appear, but then maybe they had been dealing with another incident elsewhere in the city centre. She tried to physically pull some of the people back, but no one was taking any notice. It was as though they were here to watch reality TV being filmed. With those she recognised, she used their names and pleaded, but the crowd seemed to have reverted to the level of wild men egging each other on to fight, possibly to the death. It was barbaric.

When Maggie had first signed up to serve teas in the centre of the city, she'd attended a series of training sessions. They'd had some roleplay scenarios to deal with, but until now she'd never needed or even thought about the skills they'd discussed. She knew she should call the police and get herself to safety, but in reality she guessed it would be some time before they arrived, and when they did there could well be more trouble.

She reached for her phone to call for help, but then the fight had started in earnest and people moved back out of the way. Maggie was pushed accidentally, and she dropped her phone. It fell to the ground and shattered. Instinctively she made a grab for it, but anyone could see it was useless.

Then, suddenly, while she was staring at her phone in disbelief, she felt someone grab her arm. She was twisted round as someone from behind threw his arm around her neck. She saw the glint of the knife as he shouted at the crowd to keep away.

Everything was happening so quickly,

and it all felt so unreal. The man was shouting at her. She felt the sharp knife at her throat and could see the red trickle of her blood fall onto his hand. Her heart was beating like it had never beat before, and her body had gone into a cold sweat. She could feel the man holding her tightly and she could see the crowd of people in front of her. They just stood there, watching. Why didn't anyone do anything? Why wasn't there someone trying to rescue her?

As the man held her, he felt down her body and realised she had car keys. 'Where's your car?' he breathed. She could smell the stale beer on his breath and hear the panic in his voice. She wanted to lie and tell him it was in the multi-storey car park, but he had a knife to her throat and she wasn't taking any chances.

She felt sick. For a moment she couldn't even answer. If he hadn't been holding her so tightly, she would have fallen to the ground like a ragdoll.

'That one, the Citroën,' she said,

pointing to her little car. Her voice trembled almost as much as her hand. She felt dizzy as another drop of blood landed on the pavement.

'Give me the keys,' he said.

Maggie was now too frightened to do anything other than hand over her keys and hope he'd just go away. A car could be replaced, but the thought of that knife near her face made her feel sick.

The man dragged Maggie with him to the car. He opened the boot with her keys and grabbed at her arm. 'Get in,' he said.

Maggie didn't respond at first, as she was too surprised, but he pulled on her arm and told her again to get inside the boot. Awkwardly she did as she was told, and before she knew it, the boot lid was closed and everything went black.

It seemed incredibly dark in the tiny space, but she could still hear the shouts from outside and hoped some-one would come and rescue her. Surely all those people couldn't stand by and watch her be driven away?

She heard him open the car door and felt the car lower with his weight as he got in. She knew he'd been drinking and definitely should not be driving. This only added to her panic.

For a moment she thought she was going to pass out. Again she felt sick, but tried to take control by breathing deeply and exhaling slowly. At first she found herself panting nervously, but forced herself to concentrate on getting her breathing under control, knowing she would feel better.

The one thing that kept her going was the thought of having to explain what had happened to the police and to her mother. She knew they would want as much detail as possible. She had to remember every little thing.

He roughly started the engine and the car shot back in reverse. She could hear the tyres screech as he jerked into first gear and then raced ahead at top speed.

She wondered whether anyone had

been in the way. There were still shouts and screams, presumably from the onlookers. No doubt there would be someone filming it all on their phone. Was that going to be helpful? She took another deep breath and tried to get comfortable in the confined space.

Maggie had a variety of things in her car boot. There was an assortment of carrier bags, but at least they were soft against her. She grabbed one and held it to her neck. She was still bleeding from where the knife had cut her.

There wasn't a lot of room in the boot of the car, but enough for her to be thrown this way and that. Some-where she had a first-aid kit, but that wasn't going to be much help to her in the dark.

She covered her head with her hands to protect herself from the edges of the car as she was thrown about. It was driven at top speed through the town centre. At least at this time in the evening there would be fewer people about, she thought. But although she didn't want anyone to be hurt, she did want her car to be noticed and the police informed. She wondered if the patrol car that had just parked in the layby was still there and whether they were now in hot pursuit.

She tried to work out where he was going, but she was so disorientated it was hard to follow his route. He seemed to swerve when she assumed he must be going along the main London Road, out of town. That would have been the logical thing to do, but then he'd been drinking, and perhaps he wasn't thinking in a logical way.

Maggie's senses seemed heightened in the dark space. She ignored the tight knot in the pit of her stomach and the fear of what could possibly happen next, and tried to concentrate. Her eyes were becoming more accustomed to the dark; not that there was anything much to see. She had a few things in the boot, but they were being thrown around at random, just as she was.

After a while, she thought she could

hear the faint wail of a police siren, but she wasn't absolutely sure, although she suspected that his driving would attract attention from the police as well as passers-by.

Surely someone from the Red Lion or the tea bar would have had a mobile phone and would have called the police once he'd put the knife to her neck? They must have realised it was serious and not a game.

Maggie was tossed about some more. She bumped her head and then her shoulder as the car was driven faster than it had ever been driven before.

She was sure she could now hear a police siren, or possibly an ambulance, and longed for the ordeal to stop. Then suddenly everything *did* stop. There was a loud thud and the car jerked to an abrupt halt. Maggie was thrown up and then down, and then nothing; all was strangely quiet. Her shoulder hurt. For a moment she felt as though her whole body was crumpled and broken. She felt she'd fallen apart.

Maggie waited for what seemed like an eternity. She then realised that perhaps no one would even know that she was in the boot. She began to hammer on the top of the car boot but it didn't seem to make much sound. She wondered how much air she would have and remembered a horrible story of someone suffocating in the back of a car. But just as she was beginning to become more anxious, and her breathing quickened, the boot clicked open and a very welcome light from a torch streamed in.

'Help me,' she cried.

There were police everywhere, and two ambulances. Blue lights flickered in all directions, lighting up the sky. Maggie could see what was going on, but for some reason it wasn't registering in her brain. She felt confused.

People kept asking her name. They shone lights in her eyes and told her everything was going to be all right, but nothing looked right at all. The world had gone mad.

Or was this what it was like to go insane? Was she hallucinating and seeing things? Surely this awful nightmare must stop and she'd wake up and find herself at home in bed.

One ambulance took the driver away in one direction, and the second took Maggie. Although she kept insisting she was just bruised, no one was listening to her. Perhaps they couldn't hear her over the wail of the sirens.

'I'm fine,' she kept saying, but they didn't seem to take any notice. 'Honestly, I'm just sore really; there's nothing broken. Look, I can wiggle my fingers.'

In the hospital, they kept her waiting for ages while they checked that nothing was actually broken. The police asked her lots of questions, although she felt she had little to say. She didn't know the man. She didn't know what had started the fight or why he had picked on her. Then a doctor came and gave her an injection.

'Just to calm you down,' he said.

'You're going to feel very stiff and uncomfortable in the morning, and I need to get a look at your neck. I don't think you'll need stitches, but we must get it cleaned up.'

'I only want to go home,' cried Maggie. She looked up, and there stood Cliff. At first she wondered if she was dreaming, and he'd carry her off on his white horse into the sunset. That was stupid, she decided; it must be the injection the doctor had given her. It was playing games with her mind.

'Take me home,' she begged Cliff. As she moved her arm, she winced and realised that if it was a dream, it was a very realistic one.

Cliff looked first at the doctor, and then at policeman who was guarding her bed and had already sent away two newspaper reporters.

'You can take your partner home if she has a stable night and if her neck isn't infected. Someone will need to be with her, initially at least. She'll need to rest. She's had a big shock and will probably just want to sleep, but don't leave her alone in case she's concussed. She's had a few bumps to the head.'

It was then that Maggie slipped into a deep but welcome sleep.

11

Maggie was disturbed throughout the night as the nursing staff checked on her. Cliff sat beside her, holding her hand, so he too didn't get much sleep.

The following morning Maggie woke and, as the doctor had predicted, she felt stiff and uncomfortable as if every bone in her body had been rattled. She ached and was irritated by the bandage on her neck.

'My parents will be worried,' she said.

'I called them,' Cliff told her. 'They popped in last night as soon as they'd heard, but by then you were sleeping like a baby.'

'I suppose that was a blessing. At least I wasn't talking gibberish.'

'No more than usual,' Cliff told her with a smile. Gently he squeezed her hand.

Sometime later, the doctor did his rounds. Maggie would always have a scar on her neck, but it wasn't infected. Miraculously, she'd not broken anything, but she was bruised and shocked by the whole experience. Thankfully it was agreed she could go home to sleep and to take painkillers if she felt the need.

'It's not over yet,' Cliff told her. 'The papers are after your story. I take it you don't want to do an interview?'

'I don't really want to see anyone,' Maggie admitted.

'Good. That's what we'd thought you'd say, and we've come up with a plan.'

'A plan?'

'That's right, but first things first: we have to get you out of here as quickly and as quietly as possible.'

Cliff tried to get a signal on his phone but without success.

'I need to make a quick call,' he told Maggie. 'Can you curl up and pretend you're asleep until I get back?'

Before he left the room, he handed her the alarm button to call for help. 'Press that if anyone comes in and bothers you.'

'Is that really likely?'

'Who knows? Those journalists can be pretty persistent if they smell a good story.'

Cliff disappeared to make his call. Maggie did as she was asked and pretended she was asleep. He wasn't gone long and was soon back to help her dress and get ready to leave.

'I'll be fine,' said Maggie again, but found her legs so wobbly she couldn't stand. 'I do feel a bit peculiar.'

'Hold on, I'll get a wheelchair.'

Once again he vanished. This time he seemed to be away for longer. When he returned, he was not alone. A uniformed police officer was with him.

'I'm sorry to bother you,' he said. 'I need to ask you some questions about last night. Perhaps you can start from the beginning and tell me what happened?'

Maggie did her best to remember all the details. She didn't want to have to face it all again, but knew it was something she had to do. The whole experience exhausted her, and once she'd completed her story, all she wanted to do was to go back to sleep.

'Come on,' said Cliff. 'Let's get you out of here first, then you can sleep for as long as you need.'

He said something to the policeman, who wrote down something on his notepad. Then the two of them helped Maggie into the wheelchair, and they left by a side hospital exit. Cliff wheeled her to his car and helped her in.

While he took the wheelchair to the back door, Maggie looked in the mirror and was horrified to see she had a black eye and a cut on her cheek. The cut on her neck was still covered.

'Do you really want to go home?' Cliff asked her when he returned. 'Can I take you to my home and look after you?'

Maggie nodded. There was no way

she could explain this to her mother and ever be allowed out again on her own.

'Don't worry,' he told her. 'Everything will be all right, but just now you need to rest, and hopefully you'll have more chance of peace and quiet at my place than you'll have at Haddon Hall.'

Maggie was aware of a warmth surrounding her like a security blanket as she slipped into a deep sleep. She stirred a few times and awoke, felt safe, and then slid back into her sleep.

At one point she thought she could hear a voice, Cliff's voice; but then sleep took over again, and she gave in to it. Perhaps it was whatever the doctor had given her, or maybe the painkillers were strong, or maybe it was the effects of the shock to her system. Whatever it was, the sleep was healing.

Bright sunshine streamed in through the window. Maggie stretched, but then recoiled as she realised how much she hurt. She wondered where she was. She didn't recognise the room or the big double bed she was in. It certainly wasn't a hospital ward, nor was it a familiar bedroom from home. It wasn't Angela's house either, or a hotel room.

She tried to sit up. Her clothes were on a chair by the bed. She felt her arms and then looked down and realised she was wearing what looked like a man's pair of pyjamas.

She groaned and then started as she was aware of someone else in the room who stirred.

'Maggie?' asked Cliff.

'You look terrible,' said Maggie as she took in Cliff's unshaven face and bloodshot eyes. He smiled and reached out for her hand.

'You should look at yourself in the mirror!' laughed Cliff. 'Welcome back to the land of the living.' She couldn't understand it, but he seemed to have a tear in his eye. Briskly he wiped it away.

'I feel so tired,' she said.

'You've already slept for nearly three days. I thought you'd gone into a coma, but the doctor said it was natural for you to sleep. It's all part of the shock.'

'Three days?'

'Don't worry, you didn't snore. You obviously needed it.'

Maggie smiled, pleased that he could tease her and make her laugh, even if all her muscles still ached. It even hurt to laugh.

'There was an accident?' Maggie said more to herself than to Cliff. He nodded. 'A car crash?' He nodded again. 'It was my car. Was it a write-off?'

'I should think so. I think they towed it away. I don't really know; I've been more concerned about you.'

'Thank you for all you've done.'

'Are you hungry or thirsty? I imagine you must be starving. I am,' he laughed.

Maggie wasn't sure if she was hungry or not. She was not yet thinking clearly.

Cliff went to make her a tray of food. She tried to get up, but her body felt tired and feeble. She gave up trying and just looked around at what she guessed must be his bedroom. There was a chest of drawers in front of the window and on top was a big jug of red roses.

It all started to come back to her. Cliff had come in with a bouquet of roses, red roses, and a bottle of champagne. The bottle had come from her parents.

Cliff returned a little while later with a large wooden tray piled high with food. 'It's a real mixture, because I don't know what you like, and it's just what I've got. I haven't dared leave you to go shopping, but I have done an internet shop and that's due this afternoon.'

'Thank you,' said Maggie suddenly feeling very emotional again. 'I'm very muddled. I remember being here . . .' She paused and thought for a while. 'Oh yes, then I went to the church, and . . .'

'Is that where you slept? I went to look for you, but couldn't find you. I wasn't sure if you'd have gone back to your parents' house, but I didn't dare phone them because if you weren't there, I thought they'd worry and that would make you even more cross with me.'

'I'm so sorry. I've caused such a lot of problems.'

'Nonsense,' said Cliff decisively. 'It's given me a chance to get to know you, warts and all.' Maggie blushed and looked at the pyjamas she was wearing. 'I can't say I didn't look,' admitted Cliff, 'but I didn't touch. I just wanted to make you comfortable. You're rather black and blue.'

'Thank you,' said Maggie again, and she wondered what she would have done if the tables had been turned.

They both tucked in to the food on the tray, and Maggie began to feel much better. She realised that Cliff had not eaten either.

'I didn't dare leave your side,' he said. 'You've no idea how worried I've been.'

'How did you know what had happened?' asked Maggie as she began to remember the events leading up to the accident.

'I'd been missing you, and you seemed to be avoiding me. You told me to take your belongings back home, so reluctantly I did. Your friend Angela was just leaving, and she said you were doing an extra evening serving teas in town. I had to see you. I would have been there earlier, but I had a phone call just as I left, and so I didn't get there until that madman had taken you away; but as you can imagine, there was a whole crowd of people who could fill me in on what had happened. I followed the police cars and ambulances, not knowing exactly what I'd find.'

'I don't remember you being there then.'

'No, the police wouldn't let me anywhere near you, but I could hear you saying you were fine. I just had to be patient. I followed the ambulance back to the hospital and eventually they let me see you.'

Maggie gasped as she thought of her parents. Cliff seemed to read her mind.

'Don't worry,' he said. 'I rang them as soon as I could. They'd heard about it already on the local radio but obviously didn't realise you were involved. They came as soon as they could to the hospital, but the doctor had given you something to make you sleep.'

'I'm surprised they haven't been here to nurse me, especially Mum,' said Maggie. Cliff grinned.

'That's because we had a cunning plan! You wouldn't believe how many reporters have wanted your story, even when you were still in the hospital.'

'Oh no,' cried Maggie.

'Well so far it's worked. Your mother has been a star; she's kept the curtains drawn in your room, and a stream of your friends have been visiting and feeding the press snippets of your progress. They're all camped outside Haddon Hall, where they think you are.'

Maggie smiled. 'Nice one!'

'Exactly. And it means I've been able to have you to myself, which I have to say has been wonderful, and scary.'

'Scary?'

'The responsibility! I've never even had a pet goldfish to look after, so I had no idea what it would be like to have to look after someone you care so much about.'

'Oh,' said Maggie, feeling muddled, embarrassed and excited all at once.

Cliff leaned forward and took her hand. 'I thought the other day, when you were upset and I cancelled my work so I could come back here and cheer you up, that I'd fallen in love with you. But then, when you were mixed up in that car chase and I felt I could have lost you altogether, that's when I realised just how much I do love you.'

He stroked her cheek gently, and then kissed her hand.

'Maybe you can grow to love me too, one day?' he asked.

Maggie laughed but then groaned as it hurt her bruised and cut face. 'I think I fell for you that first evening I saw you at the tea bar.'

'But I always seem to make you so

cross and annoyed,' he told her.

'That's me being cross with myself. I've been fighting all these feelings because I was so determined to be independent and live on my own and run my own business without anyone's help.'

'I'm not stopping you,' said Cliff. 'Although I might put up a fight if you try and leave me again, especially tonight.'

Maggie stretched back on his feather pillow and said, 'I don't think I ever want to leave you — not that my legs would get me very far this evening; and I haven't got a car anymore, by the sounds of it. So you're stuck with me.'

12

Maggie was now feeling much stronger, and her bruises were fading. She and Cliff had settled easily into a simple daily routine, but still he rarely let her out of his sight.

'I'm fine now,' said Maggie as she picked up a few things that Cliff had left lying around. 'I must be feeling much better, because now your untidiness is beginning to annoy me.' Cliff laughed.

'If I promise to tidy up, will you stay?'

'I can't stay forever,' laughed Maggie without really thinking what she'd said.

'Why not?' asked Cliff as if it were the simplest thing in the world for them to just carry on as they had been doing over the last few days.

'I thought you were getting uncomfortable on the sofa,' said Maggie, trying to keep the conversation light.

'Well that's easily solved,' said Cliff with a grin.

'Oh no,' said Maggie in mock seriousness. 'I like to do things properly.'

'I could suggest you have the sofa,' said Cliff, 'but I'm far too much of a gentleman.'

'Everything's happened so quickly,' said Maggie, expecting to have to put up a fight.

'You're right, and I don't want to rush you. I need you to feel the way I do. I'll be here when you want me.' Cliff squeezed her arm gently. 'But just give me a few more days of having you to myself?' he asked. 'I've planned a surprise for tonight.'

'A surprise?'

'A special meal. You didn't know I could cook, did you?'

'A man of many talents, I'm sure,' said Maggie, surprising herself at how much better she was now feeling.

'Actually, I'm glad you're up and

about today, because I've neglected my work and I need to catch up.'

'No problem. You go and do what you have to do, and I'll just potter about.'

'Make sure you have a nap if you need to,' suggested Cliff. 'I'll give you a ring later and check how you are.' He moved forward and took her in his arms. 'I want to hold you tightly and hug you, but you still seem so fragile.'

He put a finger under her chin and tilted her head back a little. His lips descended gently on hers. They were soft and warm, and yet had the power to make her melt from the tips of her toes to the top of her hair.

'Take care,' he said, and blew her another kiss from the door.

'Cliff,' called Maggie as she came to her senses, 'do you mind if I tidy up a bit?'

'Please do,' he laughed. 'I'm not really this bad, but I wasn't expecting visitors, and I've had my hands full looking after you.'

'May I also use your phone to catch up with a few people?' Maggie asked, recalling now how her phone had been broken, as well as her car.

'Help yourself,' said Cliff as he closed the door.

Maggie seemed to have a burst of energy. She felt more alive than she had ever felt before, and danced around the house putting things away and collecting her own belongings and returning them to her little bag. It all seemed so long ago when she'd first come here.

After a while, she decided to have a coffee and a rest. Although in her mind she felt alive and full of the joys of spring, her body was tired and she knew she wasn't quite 100% better.

The first call she made was to her mother. She wondered what sort of reception she would receive, but Nancy was just pleased to hear from her.

'Don't worry, Cliff's been keeping us informed, and it sounds as though you're making good progress. How's your face looking now?' Maggie was surprised he'd mentioned that to her mother.

'The bruise has nearly gone,' she said, making light of it.

'And the cut?'

'Oh, you know about that too?' said Maggie in surprise.

'I think I get more out of Cliff than I would have done from you,' said Nancy. 'I know you only try to protect me, but sometimes I worry more if I only have half the story.'

'I'm sorry,' said Maggie again. 'I seem to have made such a complete mess of everything. I've been such a fool.'

'Nonsense. I think we've all learnt a lesson or two from this episode, and we'll all be the better for it in the long run.' Nancy paused. 'And besides, it's given you a chance to get to know Cliff better. He seems very concerned about you.'

'He's been very good to me,' said Maggie.

'I know you'll come home when

you're ready, but you'll have to forgive me, there are flowers everywhere. I think we've run out of vases. I've just plonked them in water and I know you'd much rather arrange them, but I thought I'd leave that to you.'

'Thank you,' said Maggie, smiling to herself. It had always annoyed her the way her mother would just unwrap flowers and put them in water without a second thought as to their arrangement. But now it didn't really seem to matter that much at all.

As she finished the conversation with her mother and asked after her father, she realised she was very comfortable where she was now. She would have liked to have had her wardrobe full of clothes, but it was good too to curl up in Cliff's baggy jumpers and feel closer to him, even when he wasn't around.

Maggie had never considered moving in with anyone before, and yet now it suddenly seemed the right thing to do; and if she had her car and a bit more energy, she could easily have been tempted to collect her belongings and bring them back here. She was now convinced of her love for Cliff, but found it hard to show it. These feelings were so strange to her that she didn't know how to react.

As Maggie sat and finished her hot drink, she rang Dee and asked how things were going at the tea bar. It was Saturday, and Maggie had every intention of helping out as usual on Sunday.

'But my car was a write-off,' said Maggie.

'Don't worry, I can pick you up,' said Dee. 'Just tell me where you live.'

By the time Cliff came home that evening, Maggie had managed to tidy the little house.

'What's different?' asked Cliff as he opened the door.

'It's tidy,' suggested Maggie.

'No, it's been tidy before, believe me. I think somehow you've just added a feminine touch to the place that it's never had before.'

It was true: Maggie had picked some

early spring bulbs and foliage from the garden and arranged jugs of flowers in the window and on the mantelpiece. She'd set the table for their meal using a table cloth and napkins that she'd found in a drawer, still in their wrappings.

'I was going to make something for tea, but you said something about a surprise meal,' Maggie reminded him.

'That's all in hand,' said Cliff as he took off his coat and carefully hung it up, rather than putting it down on the sofa. He still wore a big grin.

'You look like a Cheshire Cat,' said Maggie.

Cliff scooped her up into his arms. 'I could get used to this,' he said. 'I never realised how good it was to come home to find you here. I've been thinking about you all day.' He kissed her and looked at her as though he were treasuring every moment.

'I don't think I'm cut out to be a cleaner,' said Maggie. 'It's exhausted me.'

'You didn't have to do it,' said Cliff as he kissed her and led her into the kitchen. 'Now you sit there while I make tea. I've got loads to tell you.'

He busied himself chopping vegetables and grating cheese to make a pasta dish.

'When you're feeling a bit better, I'll take you up to the manor and show you how they're getting on. They've made a huge difference already. I think it will be finished in a few months, and then we can start on the house.'

Maggie explained that she'd called her mum and how understanding she'd been. 'I didn't realise you'd been keeping them up to date with how I was.'

'I thought it was the best way to stop her worrying,' said Cliff. 'She's wanted to send round food parcels and goodness knows what, but I assured her I can provide for you.'

Maggie still could not believe the ease with which her overprotective mother had let Cliff step in and look after her when she obviously needed to be nursed.

'Did you tell her you were a highly qualified doctor?' asked Maggie in disbelief. Cliff just laughed.

'I think both your parents could see how I feel about you, and your friend Angela put in a good word for me.' He squeezed her hand. 'OK,' he said as he checked his watch, 'that needs to bake for about 45 minutes. I'm going to run you a hot bath and pour you a glass of wine to help you relax.'

The hot bath was wonderful. It helped soothe Maggie's shoulder, which still ached from being rocked about in her runaway car.

When she got out of the bath and returned to Cliff's room, which she was still using, she found a surprise: on his bed he'd put out her evening dress from the charity dinner. Her matching shoes and Goldstone necklace were also there.

She dressed as best she could. Cliff's room had no mirror, and the one in the bathroom was steamed up from her bath and not a full-length one like she had at home.

Maggie could hear music as she came down the old wooden stairs back into the lounge. The lights were dim. She was pleased, as it hid an ugly yellowing bruise on her arm. She could make out Cliff in his smart black suit and crisp white shirt. He offered her a glass of wine.

'Good timing. It's almost ready.'

'So you can cook,' teased Maggie as she took her first mouthful. 'This is delicious.'

'My repertoire is not very wide,' admitted Cliff. 'Can you cook?'

'I love to cook, but I don't do it very often. Mrs Timmings is Mum's housekeeper, and she prepares most of the meals, but I take over when she goes on holiday or has a day off. I love to bake cakes for the church fair and the village show — oh no!'

'What's wrong?'

'I've just remembered the jumble sale. I must have slept through it all. I'd completely forgotten about it.' Maggie also remembered her application form for the Romanian orphanage, and hoped now she wouldn't even get an interview. Angela was right — she'd be far too homesick, and it would be much better if she stuck with her teacher training idea so she could work with adults.

'Your father told me how much they'd made. I wrote it down somewhere. He said we'd know you were feeling better once you'd started to ask about things like that.'

'Don't worry; I realise I'm not indispensable. I just don't like the feeling I've let anyone down.'

'I doubt there's anyone in the village who doesn't know about your ordeal. And besides, you'd done the hard work sorting it all out beforehand,' Cliff reminded her. 'Now eat up, and then I'll take you across to the manor and show you what's been going on there.'

13

Maggie couldn't believe the progress that had been made. It already looked cleaner and more habitable.

'This side will be for the men,' said Cliff. 'It's larger, but at the moment all my clients are men. There's staff accommodation down there, and those two rooms at the end will be for the women. We can alter it if numbers change later.'

'When will people start moving in?'

'Tash is very keen, but that's a bit of a problem at the moment.'

'Oh dear, what's happened?' asked Maggie. 'I thought Emma was OK now.'

'She's fine, although she wants to get settled before the baby arrives.'

'So what's the problem?'

'I've been thinking about what you said, and so I said they can have my cottage. This place.'

'But where will we, I mean you, live?' asked Maggie. 'I'm sure you'd be welcome at Haddon Hall, but it's not on site, and I know you really want to be here.'

'Thank you for the offer, but I'll be fine. I can camp down here if necessary until we get the other house ready.'

Maggie looked in the direction of the large Victorian house which had so taken her fancy when he'd first shown her round.

'They've knocked out the window in the master bedroom and put in patio doors, but the extension to the ground floor will take a bit longer.'

'You have been busy,' said Maggie.

'It's amazing what new windows and a coat of paint can do for a place,' said Cliff. 'But the best news is that I've sorted out some work for the men, so they feel useful and able to make a contribution.'

'Great.'

'There's a stable block behind there.'

Cliff pointed. 'It's cold, but I'm told that's fine for your flowers.'

'Oh, Cliff.' Maggie put her arms around him.

'There's also a large greenhouse, so I don't know if you're any good with other plants because there's plenty of grounds to keep nice here, and we've won the contract to spruce up the old cricket pavilion on the village green.'

'I can't believe so much has happened.'

'I did a lot of work before I even met you. It's only now that it's all coming to fruition and falling into place.'

'Actually I had an idea,' said Maggie as she looked out of the window at the stables. 'Some years ago we had a cycle repair shop in the village, but when Mr Biggs retired it closed down, and now there's nowhere to go if you've got a puncture or bent handlebars, and I know it's sorely missed. Mr Biggs may even be persuaded to come out of retirement for a little while to train up some of your men.'

Cliff kissed her on the nose. 'I knew we'd work well together. Will you speak to Mr Biggs and invite him up here to see the place for himself?'

Maggie nodded and then shivered. Cliff put an arm around her.

'Come on, let's get home.'

Maggie was still dressed in her bronze evening gown. She'd borrowed one of Cliff's jackets and it was draped around her shoulders. She pulled it closer around her.

Back at Cliff's cottage, they sat down on the sofa and continued with their plans. Maggie felt warm, comfortable and safe beside the man she knew for sure that she loved. She soon fell asleep in his arms. Cliff covered her up and let her sleep.

The following day, Maggie offered to start to pack up some of his things so Tash and Em could move in. 'Are you leaving the furniture?' she asked.

'I haven't thought about that, although I doubt Tash has much furniture if any at all. But the whole place needs to be emptied, or at least cleared, so the decorators can get in, and the lounge ceiling needs re-plastering.'

'Oh well, that will keep me busy,' said Maggie. 'I'm almost back to normal,' she admitted. 'I'm sure I'll be perfectly capable of packing things up, but I wondered if my friend Angela could come over and give me a hand?'

'Whatever you want,' said Cliff.

14

Cliff kissed Maggie again before he went off for the day. Despite it being Sunday, he still had lots to do. Maggie rang Angela a couple of times but got no reply.

The place felt empty and lonely without Cliff, but Maggie tried to keep busy. She found a couple of boxes and started to wrap up a few things that she guessed wouldn't be used for a while.

When Cliff arrived home a bit later, he was surprised and then alarmed to find the place empty. He was about to phone Maggie's parents when he noticed the date on the newspaper headline and realised it was Sunday. He could guess where Maggie had gone, although didn't know how she'd managed to get transport. He suspected Angela.

Sure enough, Cliff found Maggie

busy serving teas in the cold and the drizzle in the centre of the city in the shadow of the multi-storey car park.

'Tea or coffee?' asked Maggie before she looked up. 'Oh, it's you.'

'You could have left me a note. I was worried,' explained Cliff.

'I did leave you a note,' said Maggie. 'It was in the kitchen with your tea.'

'Oh. I didn't get that far.'

'Look,' whispered Maggie. She indicated to a couple of women sitting in the bus shelter. 'That's my friend Angela and her sister.'

'Really?'

'They'd had a big row some years ago after they lost their mum. Jessie walked out and they'd not seen each other. We made all sorts of enquiries, but no one knew where she'd gone. We didn't even know if she was alive.'

'Scary.'

'Absolutely. But then I saw this young girl recently, and I knew I recognised her from somewhere. By the time I remembered who she was, I didn't know where to find her. Fortunately Angela gave me a lift tonight, and Jessie turned up for a hot meal.'

'And they were pleased to see each other?' Cliff asked.

'I held my breath. I think they were both really shocked. I hadn't said anything to Angela because I wasn't 100% sure it was Jess, and I didn't want to get her hopes up.'

There were several volunteers along with Maggie that evening as news had got round about her adventure. It had been decided that it should be safety in numbers and that they were going to enrol, en masse, for self-defence training.

'I see you've got a change of clothes,' said Cliff, looking her up and down.

'Angela collected me earlier, and I nipped home to drop off my things and change. Mum wasn't thrilled about me coming down here, so Angela promised to stay and help.'

Jess and Angela left the bus shelter and came toward Maggie and Cliff.

'Any chance you could take Maggie home?' Angela asked. 'Jess and her boyfriend are coming home with me. I can't wait to see Dad's face. It'll make his day.'

'No problem,' Cliff told her, and they waved them off.

'Well,' said Maggie, 'if I haven't achieved anything else, at least that's one or two fewer homeless people in the area.'

'So you've moved out,' said Cliff. 'That's what you said?'

'You knew I would have to, sooner or later,' said Maggie as gently as she could.

'I had hoped you'd just stay.'

'But you said yourself we needed to move out of your place and let them decorate it before Tash and Emma can move in.' Cliff nodded.

'The house isn't going to be ready for us just yet.'

'The house?'

'Well if Tash and Em are going to live in my little place, I was hoping we'd move into the bigger house. You did say you liked it.'

'I love it, but it's a family home. We don't need anything like that!'

'Wouldn't you like a family one day?' asked Cliff, and Maggie had to agree she would.

Brian took the hot water flask from Maggie. 'I realise I'm not indispensable,' she said again, and handed it over. 'Everyone managed when I was in hospital, and when I was recovering. You look cold,' said Maggie, reaching out her hand to stroke Cliff's arm as she had done many times recently. 'Are you sure you won't have a hot drink while you're here? As you can see, we're not very busy tonight. I think people are a bit wary of things at the moment.'

'OK, I'll have a coffee please,' said Cliff. 'But will you take off your gloves?'

'Cliff?' said Maggie.

'Please?'

Maggie pulled off her fingerless mittens and stuffed them in her coat pocket. Before she knew it, Cliff knelt

218

down beside her and produced a small ring box from his pocket. 'I'd intended to propose last night. That's why I cooked the special meal. But you fell asleep! Maggie,' he said seriously, 'Will you marry me and make me the happiest man ever?'

We do hope that you have enjoyed reading this large print book.

Did you know that all of our titles are available for purchase?

We publish a wide range of high quality large print books including:
Romances, Mysteries, Classics
General Fiction
Non Fiction and Westerns

Special interest titles available in large print are:
The Little Oxford Dictionary
Music Book, Song Book
Hymn Book, Service Book

Also available from us courtesy of Oxford University Press:
Young Readers' Dictionary
(large print edition)
Young Readers' Thesaurus
(large print edition)

For further information or a free brochure, please contact us at:
Ulverscroft Large Print Books Ltd.,
The Green, Bradgate Road, Anstey,
Leicester, LE7 7FU, England.
Tel: (00 44) 0116 236 4325
Fax: (00 44) 0116 234 0205

TROUBLE IN PARADISE

Tracey Walsh

When Jenna breaks up with her boy-friend and heads to St Pete Beach in Florida to collect her thoughts, she doesn't expect to find herself falling for Alex, the son of the hotel manager who she's known since she was a child. But he's already got a girl-friend — and sinister events begin to occur. Jenna receives 'asks' for her teen magazine problem page that eerily mirror her life. Someone seems to want to kill both her and Alex. And what is the connection with the deaths of Jenna's parents years ago?

LOVE'S PROMISE

Jean Robinson

Having worked the cruising circuit a number of years ago, Hannah now steps on board as a passenger, hoping for a relaxing break from her hectic life as a single parent. It's great to see some familiar faces and catch up with old friends. What she didn't bargain for was meeting her ex, and the father of her young son Charlie, on that ship! Then there's the bad-tempered Claudia, who won't leave him alone . . . Is Nick still that reckless adventurer, or could love really be lovelier the second time around?

LOST IN THE OUTBACK

Alan C. Williams

Newly qualified teacher Amy Shaw has a lot of adjusting to do when she moves from Sydney to remote Gurawang. On her first night there, someone plants an explosive in a railway wagon outside her hotel window — the first in a chain of dramatic events that colour Amy's new life. After a nearly catastrophic misstep with a handsome local banker, does she have a chance at winning the heart of the town's senior constable — and can they work together to dispel the shadows that hang over Gurawang?

SPRING AT TAIGH FALLON

Kirsty Ferry

When Angel Tempest finds out that her best friend Zac has inherited a Scottish mansion from his great-aunt, she immediately offers to visit Taigh Fallon with him. It will mean closing up her jet jewellery shop in Whitby for a few days, but the prospect of a spring trip to the Scottish Highlands is too tempting. Then Kyle, Zac's estranged and slightly grumpy Canadian cousin, turns up unexpectedly at Taigh Fallon, and events take a strange turn as the long-kept secrets of the old house begin to reveal themselves . . .

DUKE IN DANGER

Fenella J. Miller

Lady Helena Faulkner agrees to marry only if her indulgent parents can find a gentleman who fits her exacting requirements. Wild and unconventional, she has no desire for romance, but wants a friend who will let her live as she pleases. Lord Christopher Drake, known to Helena as Kit, her brother's best friend, needs a rich wife to support his mother and siblings. It could be the perfect arrangement. But when malign forces do their best to separate them, can Helena and Kit overcome the disasters and find true happiness?